"One dance."

Cassidy turned toward him, tried to brace herself for the impact of staring right into those blue eyes of his. Her heart beat faster even as sensual awareness spiked through her.

Handsome, definitely, he was. With those strong cheeks, that long blade of a nose and that chiseled jaw, the man certainly would catch the attention of most women. He even had a cleft in his chin, a cleft that softened the roughened danger edge of his features and made him even more appealing. Sexy.

His hand closed around hers as he led her onto the dance floor. Cassidy noticed that there were calluses on his fingers, and he was just so...warm.

She swallowed and held her faint smile in place as they began to dance. She tried to keep some precious distance between them but...

He pulled her even closer.

GLITTER AND GUNFIRE

USA TODAY Bestselling Author

CYNTHIA EDEN

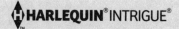

HARLEQUIN® INTRIGUE®

Recycling programs
for this product may
not exist in your area.

Thanks so much to all of my wonderful readers!
Your support is amazing!

For Denise and Dana—working with you both is
always a pleasure. Thank you, ladies!

And for my husband, Nick—where would
I be without you? Thanks for making the
last fifteen years a great ride.

ISBN-13: 978-0-373-69712-0

GLITTER AND GUNFIRE

Printed in U.S.A.

www.Harlequin.com

ABOUT THE AUTHOR

USA TODAY bestselling author Cynthia Eden writes tales of romantic suspense and paranormal romance. Her books have received starred reviews from *Publishers Weekly,* and she has received a RITA® Award nomination for best romantic suspense novel. Cynthia lives in the deep South, loves horror movies and has an addiction to chocolate. More information about Cynthia may be found on her website, www.cynthiaeden.com, or you can follow her on Twitter (www.twitter.com/cynthiaeden).

Books by Cynthia Eden

HARLEQUIN INTRIGUE

All backlist available in ebook. Don't miss any of our special offers. Write to us at the following address for information on our newest releases.

Harlequin Reader Service
U.S.: 3010 Walden Ave., P.O. Box 1325, Buffalo, NY 14269
Canadian: P.O. Box 609, Fort Erie, Ont. L2A 5X3

CAST OF CHARACTERS

CALE LANE—An ex-army ranger with a dangerous past, Cale isn't thrilled with his new assignment: guarding a society princess.

CASSIDY SHERRIDAN—Cassidy is determined to unmask a killer, even if she has to risk her own life in the process.

GENEVIEVE CHEVALIER—Cassidy's best friend, Genevieve is a pawn in a killer's deadly game. When Genevieve is taken captive, Cassidy will risk everything to save her.

BRUCE MERCER—Bruce Mercer is the director of the EOD, a man used to giving orders.

THE EXECUTIONER—A killer who has been targeting rich debutantes, the "Executioner" has eluded authorities for years. His sights now seem set on Cassidy and Genevieve. But is the Executioner also hiding a second, even deadlier agenda?

GUNNER ORTEZ—Gunner is working as Cale's backup on the latest mission, and can clearly see the danger that Cale is facing.

LOGAN QUINN—The team leader of the Shadow Agents, Logan isn't about to stand back while the lives of other agents are threatened.

Chapter One

Playing babysitter to some rich, overindulged society debutante wasn't exactly EOD Agent Cale Lane's idea of a
good time.

Give him a dense jungle, the furious blast of gunfire
and the adrenaline spike of a deadly mission any day of
the week, but stick him in a stuffy ballroom like this—

This too-posh place might as well be hell to him. But,
no, it wasn't hell—it was Carnival. Elaborate decorations
streamed from the ceiling in bursts of gold, green and
purple. The tables were covered, decked out, and the band
played on a stage that shimmered with light.

From his perch near the back wall, Cale shifted slightly
in his tux. He was supposed to be blending in with everyone else, and he was trying his best. Blending was
normally a specialty for him. He was used to being camou-
flaged on missions, but most missions weren't like this one.

Cassidy Sherridan.

His eyes narrowed on the sleek blonde. The far-too-
attractive, far-too-tempting Cassidy. He'd been sent down
to Rio de Janeiro with the express orders to watch Cassidy.

And that was exactly what he'd been doing for the past
five torturous days.

She looked up, then, her dark green eyes catching his
gaze on her. For an instant, he thought tension might have

tightened her delicate jaw, but then she smiled that slow, flirtatious smile that revealed the dimple in her right cheek.

She started walking toward him. Not that the woman walked so much as glided, and he had to admit she was sexy when she walked. No, Cassidy was sexy—period. The slit in her emerald dress parted, revealing legs that probably could have graced a runway someplace.

Her heels were high, vicious spikes, her dress was strapless, fitting her like a silken glove, and Cassidy...

She's the mission.

He couldn't let himself forget that. He hadn't been swayed by a pretty face before, and he wasn't going to start losing his cool now.

Cassidy held a champagne flute in one delicate hand. She nodded her head to a few people as she passed by them and said a couple of polite words while keeping her perfect smile in place. Some of the other guests were decked out in their Carnival masks. The celebration was going full swing in Rio. Earlier, Cassidy had even worn a small, delicate eye-mask.

The mask was gone now.

And she was right in front of him.

Still smiling faintly, she said, "You know, it would probably help things considerably if you stopped looking as if you were being tortured as you stood over here."

He'd been tortured a few times. Memories that he didn't want to relive, right then.

"It's a party," she continued in that husky voice that reminded him too much of dark bedrooms. "Not a prison."

What would she know of prison? Or torture? Cale cocked a brow and let his gaze sweep over her. Cassidy Sherridan was a mystery to him. A gorgeous, too-fancy mystery. Her blond hair was swept back in a twist, the style accentuating her high cheekbones and those deep green eyes that made him think of things a soldier should *not* be thinking about.

Her nose was delicate, her chin a little too pointed. Her skin was flawless, golden, and she—

She was trying to distract him.

"Don't you have admirers to entertain?" he asked, his voice a rough growl, one that was a direct contrast to the softness of Cassidy's voice.

She laughed lightly. "And here I believed that I was entertaining an admirer. The way you've been staring at me all night…actually, for the past few days, it made me think that I did have an admirer in you." Now it was her turn to study him. Her gaze sharpened. "Why have you been following me?"

Her scent, light, sweet, seemed to fill the air around them. "Sorry, ma'am," he drawled, letting his Texas accent slip out deliberately. He'd long ago learned how to ditch and retrieve that accent at will. "But I think you have me confused with someone else."

Cassidy shook her head. "No, I think it would be very hard to confuse a man like you with anyone else." Her smile was still in place, but a brittle edge had entered her voice. Then, surprising him, she stepped forward. Her arms came up, as if she were hugging him, and he responded instinctively, wrapping his own arms around her.

Cassidy's body was slender and warm against his. Because of her high heels and the fact that Cassidy's own height skirted just above five foot eleven, their mouths were close. Temptingly close.

But she didn't kiss him. She pushed up onto her toes. Her mouth slipped toward his left ear, and she whispered, "Stop tailing me before you ruin everything."

He stiffened at her words and at the sudden hard jolt of arousal that knifed through him. Her breath blew lightly against his ear. His fingers tightened around her waist. To onlookers, Cale knew it would appear that they were embracing but, holding her this tightly, he felt the hard tension in Cassidy's body.

Cassidy Sherridan was furious with him.

"I don't care who sent you." She whispered the words. He felt her lips press lightly against his ear. His body hardened. Then she said, "The last thing I need is an EOD agent in my way."

An EOD agent. She *did* realize who—what—he was, and that was some very surprising news, mostly because there were only a few people in the world with enough clearance to know about the Elite Operations Division. According to the U.S. government, the EOD didn't exist.

Not officially, anyway.

The Elite Operations Division operated far below the radar. The EOD agents had all been hand selected by Bruce Mercer, the man who seemed to *be* the EOD. The agents went out on the most deadly missions. They took the cases that others—in the *official* U.S. agencies—couldn't handle. Their very success and survival depended on the EOD's secrecy.

But this woman, who went to a series of parties, night after night, barely sliding into her hotel room past dawn, this woman with a dozen admirers always close to her, this woman who seemed to burn through ridiculous amounts of money in mere moments… *She* knew about the EOD?

So much for secrecy.

Her fingers pressed against his shoulders as Cassidy leaned back to study him once more. "I didn't catch your name."

Because he hadn't given it to her.

"But maybe that's for the best," she added with a little nod. "Since this is the end of our acquaintance."

No, it wasn't even close to the end.

"When I walk away in a moment, I expect you to do the same," Cassidy told him.

The woman was giving him orders? Almost cute.

"Head to the back door. It's ten feet on your right. Go down the stairs there. That's the entrance and exit used by the staff at this event. None of the guests will notice when you leave."

Ah, yes, she *was* giving him an order. And it wasn't as cute anymore.

"I don't want to see you again." She was smiling as she said it, but her eyes had hardened. "Don't get in my way."

Then she turned and walked away.

Interesting.

His gaze slid over the slender column of her back. Far too much skin—such golden, perfect skin—was revealed by the plunging back of her gown.

She didn't look at him. Just headed over to a pretty red-head, and the two women immediately started talking, their voices seemingly happy and light.

Cale realized that Cassidy Sherridan had just dismissed him.

He wasn't the type of man to be dismissed.

When he had a mission, he executed that mission. An angry debutante wasn't about to get in *his* way.

Cale glanced toward the exit she'd indicated, then right back to her.

With a faint smile curving his lips, he started to stalk his prey.

VOICES ROSE AND FELL around her, and Cassidy tried hard to focus through the rumble—and to ignore the wild pounding of her heart.

He's gone. You're in control. You have this—

"Um…Cassidy?" Her friend Genevieve Chevalier's voice had dropped, so Cassidy had to lean closer to hear her words in the crush of people. "Who is that delectable man coming after you?" A light French accent brushed her words.

Cassidy blinked at her. Wait, had Genevieve just said… *coming after…?*

Cassidy locked her back teeth even as she gave a smile, the same fake smile that she'd grown used to offering people in the past year. "I'm sure I don't know who you're talking about." She laughed lightly. "But then, this room is full of delectable men."

Not that she paid those men much notice. Ever since she'd arrived at the charity ball, she'd been totally focused on *him.*

She glanced over her shoulder, following Genevieve's gaze. The man in question should have been heading toward the exit. The stranger—the guy with the dark blue eyes, the hard jaw, the face that she found both dangerous and sexy—was striding toward her.

He was tall, around six foot three, with wide shoulders. She'd first noticed him three days ago—mostly because it was hard to ignore a man like him. Especially with that dark intensity that seemed to pulsate off him.

The day she'd noticed him for the first time, they'd been at another party, another glittering ballroom, one decked out in the familiar gold-and-purple colors of Carnival. He'd been leaning against the back wall there, too, watching her.

But not with lust in his eyes, the way others sometimes did.

Instead, cold calculation had filled his stare.

"He seems very taken with you," Genevieve murmured. With an effort, she kept her smile in place. He should have *taken* himself out of there. Like she couldn't spot an EOD agent a mile away.

Deliberately, she looked away from him, making a point of giving the man her back. *Take a hint.* The band started to play again, a slow, romantic tune, and some of the chatter quieted just as—

A hand closed over her shoulder. Warm, strong, his. Every muscle in Cassidy's body tightened in response to that touch.

"I want this dance." His words were rough, a demand, certainly not the suave invitation that most of the men at this event would have offered her.

But, then, he wasn't most men.

Genevieve stood watching them, her golden eyes wide.

Cassidy realized the stranger hadn't given her much choice. She could refuse, then Genevieve—glorious gossip that she was—would want to know why. The point had been to make the mysterious man vanish, not to pull him into her life even more.

He'd obviously missed the point.

"One dance," she agreed softly, inclining her head in what she hoped appeared to be a gracious move.

She'd be sure he got the point this time.

Cassidy turned toward him, tried to brace herself against the impact of staring right into those blue eyes of his. But there was no bracing that would be good enough. Each time she looked into his eyes, her heart beat faster even as sensual awareness spiked through her.

Handsome, he definitely was. With those strong cheeks, that long blade of a nose and that chiseled jaw, the man certainly would catch the attention of most women. He even had a cleft in his chin, a cleft that softened the roughened edge of his features and made him even more appealing.

His hand closed around hers as he led her onto the dance

floor. Cassidy noticed that there were calluses on his fingers, and he was just so…warm.

She swallowed and held her faint smile in place as they began to dance. She tried to keep some precious distance between them but—

He pulled her even closer.

Annoying.

"I told you to leave," she gritted out through her locked teeth.

His lips twitched. "Um, you did. But I decided that I wanted to stay."

He was moving easily, fluidly, a bit surprising for a man of his size. A solider who knew how to dance—and dance well, she realized, as he gave her a little spin and dip.

Her lips parted as she pulled in a quick breath. Then he was moving her again, leading her around the dance floor.

His gaze dropped to her mouth. It seemed to heat. "I think—" his voice was deep, rolling "—that you owe me an explanation."

Her brows climbed. "What?" She didn't owe him anything. They didn't know each other. As soon as the dance ended, their association would end, too.

"Tell me about the EOD," he said. Cassidy realized that he'd just used her trick. When he'd said those words, he'd put his lips right next to her ear and whispered his demand.

Only…had his lips pressed lightly against her ear? It felt as if they had. And his tongue. Had he…licked her? She certainly hadn't…licked…him.

Had she?

Goose bumps rose on her arms. "I don't need to tell you anything."

Really, Mercer had stooped to this level? Sending a new babysitter after her? He'd promised the last agent was it. It looked like he'd broken another promise.

Same story, different day. She should have expected this from him.

"You think I work for something called the EOD," the man told her. She pulled back, staring up at him. His hair was dark, thick, and her fingers were brushing against the nape of his neck.

Why were her fingers doing that? She immediately flattened them against the back of his tux.

"Shouldn't you at least tell me what the EOD is?" he pressed.

Cassidy sighed. "Cut the act, okay? I've seen your dossier picture. I know you're an agent." That was how she'd first recognized him at the other party. She had a thing about faces. Once she saw one, she never forgot it.

Actually, there were quite a few things that she couldn't forget.

His jaw hardened just a bit. "Well, I'm at a disadvantage—"

"Yes, you are," she interrupted him, making sure that her voice stayed low so that none of the other dancers would overhear. "Because you've been sent down here for no reason. I *don't* need you."

The song ended. Thankfully. Blessedly.

She tried to pull away from him.

He didn't let her go.

"Are you sure about that?" he asked.

"Yes," she hissed. "I'm sure. I'm perfectly fine. This place is safe—"

A scream cut through the ballroom. At the high-pitched, desperate sound, everyone froze.

Cassidy's blood iced. *Genevieve.* That had been her scream. She *knew* Genevieve's scream.

Cassidy's gaze flew to the right as she looked for her friend. There, near the staircase. One glance and Cassidy knew why her friend had screamed. Men in black—men wearing ski masks and armed with handguns—surrounded Genevieve. One man had a gun to her side. The other three men were fanning out, advancing toward the unarmed guests.

"Anyone moves," the man holding Genevieve shouted, "I kill her." No accent covered his words.

Cassidy's breath heaved in her lungs. No, no, this could not be happening now. It shouldn't be happening—not to Genevieve!

But it *was* happening. She was staring at a nightmare straight from her past. The armed men swept into the crowd.

And—

"Cassidy Sherridan!" the man holding Genevieve shouted. "We want her."

Cassidy took a step forward.

Only to be halted by the man who was quickly becoming the bane of her existence.

"Too bad," the EOD agent whispered—a whisper that reached only Cassidy's ears. "Because I'm not letting them get you."

He didn't understand what was happening. She did. She was also more than ready to trade herself for Genevieve.

So while everyone else was frozen, she jerked away from the agent and called out, "You want me? I'm right here."

The agent swore.

The masked man shoved Genevieve away and began closing in on Cassidy. His gun was aimed dead center at her chest.

Cassidy lifted her chin and waited.

Only in the next second she wasn't staring at the

gun. The EOD agent had grabbed her and pushed her behind him.

No!

"Don't play hero," the masked man snarled. "It's a sure-fire way to end up dead."

"That's a chance I'll take," the agent drawled, letting his Texas accent slip in once more as he pulled out his own weapon. A gun she hadn't even noticed when they'd been dancing.

The men in masks inched closer as everyone else in the room started to rush for the doors.

So much for everyone freezing. *I'm the one they want.*

And if tall, dark and handsome hadn't just tried to be a white knight, the gunmen would have gotten her.

The EOD agent had just ruined her plans.

"FOUR MEN, ALL ARMED," Logan Quinn murmured into his mouthpiece as he kept his eyes on the scene unfolding before him. His fingers tightened around the binoculars. He sure hadn't been expecting the attack to be so public.

There were at least a hundred civilians in that ballroom. Some very well-connected civilians with pull in too many countries to count. If the gunmen started firing...

We can't let that happen.

"It's time for us to go in," Logan said, knowing that the man listening to his comm feed would be ready to attack. Gunner Ortez was always ready.

Now, if Cale Lane would just get the pretty blonde out of harm's way, then the Shadow Agents could attack.

"THERE ARE FOUR of us," the gunman growled, "and only one of you. It's a bad night to play hero."

Cale kept his weapon up and ready. Chaos surrounded him, and while most of the people were running for any exit they could find, Cassidy hadn't so much as budged an inch behind him. The woman *should* have fled for safety.

She also shouldn't have offered herself up as a willing sacrifice. They'd deal with that part later.

After he got rid of the gunmen.

"What makes you so sure I'm alone?" Cale asked. The ballroom, with all of its windows that looked out over the city—well, it sure allowed plenty of people the opportunity to look back in. "Drop your weapons," Cale ordered. "*All* of you—drop them while you still have the chance."

Laughter. He'd expected that. They'd foolishly think that he was bluffing. They'd find out, too late, that he wasn't.

The laughter died away. The guy's finger began to tighten around the trigger as he took aim at Cale. "Mister, you're dead."

No, he wasn't.

Cale shot his own weapon, firing right at the man in black. The two shots blasted almost simultaneously.

More screams. More shouts.

More chaos.

Cale grabbed Cassidy and rushed toward the exit—the back door that she'd tried to get him to take earlier. The gunman's bullet had grazed his side, barely scraping him, while his own had sunk into the man's right shoulder.

Aiming wouldn't be so easy for the guy now.

"No!" Cassidy yelled as she dug in her heels. "Stop! I can't leave!"

Yes, she could. Staying wasn't an option for her. His mission—his assigned duty—was to protect her.

When she tried to break free of his grip and run back toward the gunman, Cale just held her tighter. Then he lifted her over his shoulder.

"What are you doing?" She kicked him, hard, her heels coming close to his new wound. "Let me go!"

Why? Hell, the woman must have a death wish.

Figured.

Gunfire exploded. *Rat-a-tat.* Ah, the sound he was so familiar with...only they weren't in a jungle, and the civilians weren't safe.

I need cover, here...come on...come on...

His team was out there, lurking in the shadows. An EOD agent didn't head into a mission without support, even a strange mission like this one.

Logan Quinn and Gunner Ortez were out there. They would have his back, they would—

Logan burst into the ballroom. He didn't fire his weapon. Logan just launched right at one of the masked men.

As he hesitated at the staff exit, Cale's gaze swept the room. Another masked man was aiming his gun at the redhead, the woman who'd been talking with Cassidy earlier. The man looked like he was about to kill her—

But a bullet hit him instead. A bullet that hadn't come from *inside* the ballroom.

Instead, it had burst through the window on the far left, shattering the glass. Cale knew exactly who'd fired the shot.

Gunner. The ex-SEAL sniper never missed a target.

His cover was there.

Now, time to get the lady *out*.

Cale kicked out with his foot, throwing open the exit. Others had already started down the narrow staircase. Cassidy was screaming. Yeah, what a way to show her appreciation.

Hell was breaking loose behind them. He just needed

to get her to safety, then he could go back and help Gunner and Logan contain the scene.

He made it down to the first floor, easily holding his struggling captive.

As soon as he stepped out of the stairwell, Cale saw security guards rushing forward. *Better late than never, huh?* At least they'd finally decided to join the party.

He thrust Cassidy at one of them. "Take care of her!"

Cassidy yanked free. "I don't need taking care of!" Her hair had come loose. It tumbled around her shoulders. With her flushed cheeks, glittering eyes and that wild mane of hair, she didn't look so ice-princess perfect anymore.

It grated but…she was even more beautiful that way.

The guard who'd held Cassidy for all of three seconds started stuttering. Cale ignored him and leaned in close to Cassidy. "If you want to keep living, you'll stay down here. Stay with the guards, and I'll take care of the men upstairs."

Only…was that smoke coming from upstairs? Hell, it was. And when he strained, he could hear the crackle of flames.

The stampede for the main door became even wilder as everyone caught the scent in the air. The security guards didn't stay to help Cassidy. They fled.

Everyone fled.

Everyone but Cale.

And Cassidy.

Actually, that crazy woman tried to go back *up* the stairs. He caught her arm and yanked her against him. *Death wish.* He pulled out the small transmitter that would connect him to the other agents. "What the hell is going on up there?" Cale demanded.

"Leave the scene," Logan's voice immediately blasted

back. "Two attackers are dead. The others retreated but left a fire in their wake."

Not the news he wanted to hear.

Cassidy kept trying to run for the stairs. The woman was trying to drive him insane.

"Come on!" He locked his arm around her stomach and pulled her back against him.

"No! My friend is up there! Genevieve! Gen—"

Other people were rushing down the service stairs. They were about to be crushed.

He could hear sirens blasting. More help, coming as quickly as they could.

"Ballroom is clear," Logan barked. "Get the target *out.*"

When the team leader gave an order, you didn't question him. Cale picked Cassidy up into his arms and carried her out.

"No!" Cassidy yelled. "Genevieve, I need—"

"She's clear!" They were outside. Fresh air hit him. He glanced back. Saw the flash of flames in the upstairs windows. And...saw the shadow of a man dropping down the side of the building.

Logan. Rappelling down.

Had the gunmen used the same method of escape?

And why had they targeted—

"Cassidy!"

When he heard the cry, Cale's hold tightened on Cassidy. But the woman calling her—that was the redhead. Cassidy's friend.

"Genevieve?" Cassidy whispered, voice breaking with hope.

Cale's gaze swept the scene. Men and women in their fancy gowns and their tuxes now stood, shaken, in the shadows, as they stared up at the burning building.

A night of fun, now a night of fear.

"Let me go," Cassidy told him. "Please."

He eased her to her feet. She'd lost her high heels some-place, and her bare feet pressed into the cement. Cale stared into her eyes.

He wasn't letting her go. Not really.

But for now, he *would* let her walk away.

Cassidy turned from him. She hurried away. Her hands locked around her friend as she held Genevieve tight. Genevieve was talking quickly in French.

Since he spoke French as easily as he did English, Cale understood her words and her frantic fear that *mort* had almost taken them both.

But, no, Cale hadn't been about to let death get close to Cassidy.

He eased back from the scene, keeping Cassidy in his sights. More of the local authorities arrived, rushing fran-tically to the rescue.

With Carnival in swing, this was the last thing that the powers-that-be in Rio would want. An attack on wealthy tourists? No way would they want that bit of info leaking to the media.

Medics were checking out the shaken men and women.

Logan was in the shadows, scanning the area. Cale saw him, but he doubted that anyone else noticed the other agent.

They were all too busy dealing with the fear and the fire.

A fire that was still spreading. Still slowly destroying the historic building.

The gunmen had seemingly vanished.

They'd come for Cassidy.... Would they try to return for her?

His hand clenched as he remembered her walking to-ward the masked man.

Yes, he realized, they would come for her, but he would make absolutely sure that they'd find him standing in their way.

Cassidy looked up, then, and her gaze met his. So much emotion was in her eyes, blazing just as brightly as the flames. Anger, no, fury…and fear.

He forced his hands to unclench as he watched her. Soon, he would have her alone, and when he did, he would discover all of her secrets.

Every. Last. One.

He would find out just why armed men had stormed the party looking for her.

And he'd learn just how the rich debutante knew all about the most covert group of agents currently working for the U.S. government.

Cale was quickly realizing that there was a whole lot more to Cassidy Sherridan than he'd initially realized.

The woman could prove to be very, very dangerous.

Chapter Two

She wasn't alone.

Cassidy had just taken a few steps into the darkened interior of her hotel bedroom when she realized that someone was waiting in the shadows.

She froze, her hands by her sides, as she tried to decide if she needed to flee—or fight.

"Relax," came a rough voice from the darkness, a voice that she recognized instantly. Not many men sounded like danger and desire growling all at once. *He* did. "If I saved you before, would I really come back now to hurt you?"

Those weren't reassuring words. "You never know," she said softly. Her fingers lifted, and she tightened the belt of her robe, making sure that she was covered. Judging by his voice, he had to be on the left-hand side of the room. She turned her head, narrowing her eyes as she strained to find him in the dark.

"I was sent down here with strict orders."

Her eyes adjusted a bit, and she could just see him, sitting in her heavy leather chair. She was in one of the bigger suites offered by the hotel. A suite that should have been secure, but the agent had certainly gotten entrance easily enough.

Now he was lounging in her bedroom. He'd just made

himself comfortable. "Do your 'orders' include breaking into my bedroom?" Mercer wouldn't have gone that far.

Would he?

"I'm supposed to keep an eye on you. Supposed to keep you safe." He paused a beat. "But you already know that, just as you seem to know so very much about—"

"The EOD?" Cassidy supplied in what she thought was a rather helpful way.

Silence was her answer.

But silence was pretty much the norm when it came to the EOD.

She sighed. "Look, uh, Agent, I—"

"Cale."

Cassidy frowned, not that he could see her frown in the dark.

"My name's Cale Lane."

The words could be a lie. Other EOD agents had given her false names before. "All right, fine, Cale." She headed toward him, her steps angry, a little too hard, but their sound was swallowed by the thick carpeting. "We're ending this farce right now."

She'd get Mercer on the phone. He could call off his attack dog.

"Why were those men after you?"

He didn't know?

Her steps slowed.

"Two men died tonight," he continued. "Two men who seem to have no identities. Their fingerprints had been burned away, and, so far, no one can figure out a single thing about their pasts."

Her mouth was getting dry. "The EOD can figure out plenty. Just give them time."

"Are you part of the EOD?"

He seemed so doubting that it was actually insulting.

But she bit her lip before she snapped back a response at him. He obviously thought she was nothing but a piece of fluff, flitting around from party to party.

After all, wasn't that exactly what she'd been doing for the past week, ever since she'd arrived in Rio? One party after another.

But that was her cover. What she was *supposed* to do.

Pity no one ever actually looked beneath her cover appearance.

Not even Mercer.

"I stood between you and a bullet tonight," Cale said. His voice seemed even rougher, and it sent a shiver over her. "Don't you think that entitles me to some explanations?"

No, she didn't. "I don't remember telling you to stand there." Actually, if he hadn't gotten in her way, then she would have *finally* made the headway that she needed on this case. Instead, he'd gotten all tough and alpha male, and she'd had to act defenseless as he'd carried her away.

If she'd fought him too hard, if she'd broken free, then all that she'd worked for would have been destroyed in an instant.

He rose slowly, a lethal shadow that came toward her with slow, stalking steps. She refused to retreat from him, but when he closed in, every cell in her body flashed on high alert.

Being near him made her feel too on edge.

Too aware.

She shoved back that awareness. Locked it deep inside.

"Two men got away tonight," Cale told her. "Doesn't that worry you?"

Yes. "No."

"Liar."

He seemed so sure. No one had seen past her lies before, so why would he be any different? "I want you out of my room."

He didn't move.

Fine. She skirted around him, made it to her nightstand and grabbed the smart phone there. One press of her fingers and— "Mercer?" she said when the EOD's director answered the call. "What have you done now?"

She heard Cale's sharp inhale.

"You've got the EOD director on speed dial?" he asked, seemingly shocked.

On speed dial? Um, something like that.

"Your agent is going to ruin everything," she said, her words tumbling out. "I don't know if you've heard about what happened tonight, but—"

"I heard." Mercer's flat voice, completely devoid of emotion, cut through her frantic speech. "I heard, and that's exactly why Cale Lane is staying with you."

Her fingers tightened around the phone. "If he's here—"

"Then nothing will happen to you," Mercer told her. "Cale is one of the best agents I've got. No one will get to you while he's on guard."

If no one could get to her…*then how am I supposed to complete my mission?* Only, Mercer didn't think she had a mission. Mercer thought she needed to be coddled. Protected.

That she wasn't strong enough to face the dangers in the world.

Wrong. Mercer didn't know her very well. "This is a mistake." She fought to keep her own voice as emotionless as his. Impossible. Emotion always ruled her.

Never him.

Hadn't she learned that lesson long ago?

"No. This is your life, and I won't risk it." There was

no give in his voice at all. "While you're in Rio, Cale Lane stays with you."

She was going to break the phone. In her mind, Cassidy could see it splintering beneath her hand into a dozen pieces. "If that's what you want…" Because he *always* got what he wanted. When would she ever get what she wanted? Not bothering with any more words, Cassidy ended the call. After all, there was nothing else to say.

Her fingers trembled.

Cassidy turned toward Cale. She needed to phrase this right, in order to match up with the conversation she'd just had. Cassidy cleared her throat. "Mercer agreed that he'd made a mistake. Your services are no longer—"

Her phone rang.

Cale reached for her hand and pried open her fingers. He took her phone.

"Sir?" he said, and she knew he was talking to Mercer.

"Yes, she's right here."

Then he leaned forward and turned on the bedside lamp. She flinched when the light hit her. The sudden flow of light should have made Cale look less intimidating.

It didn't.

She could see the hard edge of his jaw and the intense lines of his face. "I'll stay with her. Every minute."

The hell he would.

After a few more moments, Cale ended the call and stared down at her.

Emotions wanted to rip Cassidy apart right then. All of her hard work, for so long…*for nothing.*

"Mercer just promised me a briefing at 0600," he said as his assessing gaze drifted over her. "You really going to make me wait until then in order to find out what's going on with you?"

Not much time. "What's going on is that I'm working

a case, and your presence here jeopardizes its success."
Truth.

"Mercer doesn't think so."

That was because Mercer didn't think she could handle things on her own.

"And you know the director…" Cale continued, rolling his shoulders as if pushing away a heavy burden. "When that SOB says jump, we're all supposed to learn how to fly."

Her breath rushed from her lungs. *He doesn't realize who I am.* Cale had obviously decided that she was, indeed, another EOD agent.

Not quite, cowboy. Not quite. And he did remind her of a cowboy. Maybe it was that Texas drawl that slipped out every now and then. Maybe it was the hard edge that clung to him. The tough exterior.

But she was thinking of him as cowboy tough and he—he was thinking of her as the spoiled debutante. It grated, but as long as he didn't realize exactly who she was, then his guard would stay lowered.

She'd had plenty of babysitters—um, bodyguards—over the past few years. She'd gotten pretty adept at handling them.

And dodging them.

Since Cale didn't realize her true identity, that would make things even easier for her.

She smiled at him. A real smile.

He blinked. A furrow appeared between his dark brows.

"I think we got off on the wrong foot." Cassidy even offered him her hand. Why not be friendly? That would help to make him feel even more at ease with her. "It looks like we'll be…close…for the next few days, so maybe we should just start fresh."

They'd be close until she could manage to ditch him

and go after those gunmen on her own. They were in the city. Pinpointing their next attack area had been the tricky part. Now that she knew they were in the general area, she just had to track them.

Cale silently regarded her offered hand, the hand that was still hovering in the air between them. She wiggled her fingers.

His own hand lifted and finally closed around hers. Well, swallowed hers was probably a better description. Cale used his grip to pull her closer to him.

Caught off balance by that stronger-than-expected hold, she had to take a few quick steps forward.

She was suddenly way too conscious of her thin robe and of the fact that she had nothing on beneath that robe.

Had he noticed?

The gleam of awareness in his eyes said he had.

Oh, boy.

"Partners?" Cale murmured.

She nodded. He could believe that they'd be partners for a bit. A few precious hours remained before dawn and Mercer's promised briefing. She could fool him until then, and surely she'd manage to slip away in that time.

"Partners don't keep secrets from each other," he continued.

He hadn't let go of her hand.

Mere inches separated their bodies.

"Tell me about the case."

His fingers slowly freed hers.

She took the breath that her starving lungs so desperately needed.

"I'm working on an abduction case." Again, mostly true. And to think that Mercer believed she spent her days just spinning lies. There was *some* truth to her existence. Cassidy thought the best way to deceive was to use a mix of truth and lies. "Those men tonight, they took someone else a while back."

More truth. A painful one, at that.

"Who?"

Before she did this "baring of the soul" bit, she'd really prefer putting on some clothes. If her soul was going to be exposed to him, then her flesh could at least be covered more. "Do you mind if I get dressed?" The question was supposed to be flippant.

Instead, her voice came out hoarse and soft and inviting.

She hadn't meant it to be that way. Yes, Cale Lane was attractive—sexy and compelling in that dark and dangerous way of his—but she wasn't interested in him. Was she?

Maybe.

Yes.

If they'd met in a different time. Different place.

Okay, maybe an entirely different life.

"You don't have to dress on my account," he told her. The hint of Texas was back in his voice, thickening the words.

"I'd better dress on my own account." Because being mostly naked in front of the agent wasn't a good plan.

Mercer would be furious.

So, what?

She held Cale's gaze a moment longer, then scurried around him and headed for her closet. She fumbled quickly inside, grabbing her jeans and a T-shirt. "I'll change in the bathroom and be right back." She didn't glance over her shoulder at him as she hurried into the relative safety of the bathroom.

She did turn the lock into place.

Snick.

Then she dressed as quickly as she could…before hurrying toward the window—and escape. She'd picked the hotel deliberately. She wasn't staying there because of the five-star dining options or the perfect proximity to some of the main Carnival events.

She was in that hotel because it offered suites that were housed on the second floor—a floor full of balconies. And, so convenient for her, there was even an old-style lattice on the side of her building. Lattice that she could use in her bid for freedom.

Cassidy believed in the value of an escape plan. Because plans like that…they sure came in handy during situations exactly like this one.

THEY HADN'T GOTTEN their target. Ian Gagnon glared at the men around him. It should have been so simple. Those rich fools had been too afraid to fight back.

The plan had been perfect.

Slip into the party.

Grab the girl.

Get away.

They'd done the same routine a dozen times, all without any mistakes. But this time, with *her,* everything had gone to hell. They'd had to fight their way to safety.

Two of his men hadn't made it out of that fire.

They'd fallen to gunfire.

Gunfire.

The party hadn't just been filled with helpless fools. The man who'd come so quickly to Cassidy Sherridan's rescue—her possessive lover with the glittering gaze and the gun holstered under his tux—he was a threat that Ian had not anticipated.

But the man was a threat that could be eliminated.

He would study that mysterious gentleman. Learn his secrets and weaknesses. Everyone had weaknesses that could be exploited. Ian knew that well.

Cassidy's lover hadn't been alone in the ballroom. Another man had come to his aid, fighting, battling viciously. And a third person—a shooter, a sniper—had fired on Guan. The bullet had flown through the window and taken Guan's life. Guan had been a valuable part of Ian's crew. Strong, cruel, able to kill so easily—he'd been a key asset.

And he'd been caught unaware.

At least three men. All centered on Cassidy? It certainly seemed that way.

He'd get to her, but first, he'd have to separate Cassidy from her circle of protectors.

Or he'd have to simply kill those protectors. Payback, for the lives of his men.

He'd always believed in the value of an eye for an eye.

CALE WASN'T A FOOL. Cassidy might think he was misled by a wide smile and flirting eyes—and a very short robe—but this wasn't his first case. He wasn't some green soldier who'd be distracted by a pretty face. Or long legs.

So when Cassidy came shimmying down the lattice outside of her hotel, he was waiting for her.

The shadows hid him. All of the agents in his team knew how to use the shadows. So he stood in the darkness, watching her jump from the lattice and touch down gracefully on the cement. She was almost bouncing with excitement.

You thought you got away from me?

Not even close.

She glanced back up at the open bathroom window as she eased away from the building. She still hadn't seen him.

Time to change that.

He stepped forward, moving soundlessly, the way he'd

learned to hunt when Uncle Sam had first trained him to be an army ranger.

She still didn't hear him.

And she was an EOD agent? Doubt gnawed at him. Cassidy sure didn't act like an agent.

He reached out and curled his fingers around her shoulder.

Cassidy screamed.

Not like an agent.

An agent would attack first, not scream.

But Cassidy's attack came seconds after her scream. She whirled around, striking out at him with a strong left hook. It would have been a good blow, if it had connected to his face.

It didn't.

He caught her fist in his hand, freezing the blow. "Did you need some air?" Cale murmured, trying to sound mildly curious.

A shaft of streetlight fell on her face, and he saw her surprise as her jaw dropped open.

"Because, if you needed some air—" Cale shrugged "—I would have been happy to go for a walk with you. You should have just asked me."

She tried to jerk back her fist. Because there was no place for her to run in that narrow alleyway, he let her go.

Cassidy was caged between him and the side of the hotel. Freedom wasn't in sight.

He crossed his arms over his chest and waited, sure that whatever lie was about to spill from her full lips would be interesting.

"I didn't expect you to be waiting." She cocked her head as she studied him. Cassidy rocked forward onto the balls of her feet. "You must have come down here the minute I shut the bathroom door."

Yes, he had. Cale wondered why she wasn't trying to lie to him.

"How did you know?" Cassidy asked. "You *shouldn't* have known."

She looked quite different from the glittering debutante who'd been in the ballroom. Different from the seductive temptress in the silk robe who'd made him ache minutes before.

Problem.

Because he wasn't supposed to want her. That hadn't been part of his assignment. He'd never mixed business with pleasure before.

Don't start now.

"How did you know I was going to run?" Cassidy pressed. Nervous energy seemed to pour from her.

"Because Mercer told me that you would run." *If you let her out of your sight, she's gone,* had been Mercer's gruff words. He hadn't actually believed the man, at least, not until she'd said...

I'll change in the bathroom and be right back.

"And your voice changed," he said. A small hitch, barely noticeable, but he'd been paying careful attention to her. That little hitch had put him on high alert.

He'd known that Cassidy wasn't coming back to him.

So he'd decided to go after her.

"My voice changed?" Her voice rose then. "Impossible. *No one* can tell when I'm lying."

He flashed a hard smile. "I could."

She frowned at him; then her gaze snaked over his shoulder. *Ah, nice trick.* Her eyes had narrowed even more, as if she was intently studying something behind him. Obviously, the lady was trying to distract him. If he followed her gaze and looked in that direction, she'd try to run away.

This wasn't amateur hour. He wasn't about to—

"Look out!" Cassidy screamed.

She didn't try to run away.

She grabbed him, twisting with him so that they both fell in a heap, crashing onto the cement even as a crack of thunder broke the waning night.

Not thunder. He knew that sound too well—*gunshot.*

He rolled them, positioning their bodies so that he was on top of her, shielding Cassidy. He heard her mutter, "You're welcome, cowboy."

He lifted his gun. His gaze searched the area. The shot had come from the south, from the heavier shadows there. They had no good cover, and he had to get her out of there.

From what he could tell, the shot hadn't drawn any attention. They were away from the main party streets, so this area of town was pretty deserted. And the shooter— well, he was probably just waiting for Cale and Cassidy to move.

They'd rolled behind an old sports car. One that they couldn't hide behind forever. But some generous person had conveniently parked the car at the edge of the alley.

Your mistake, buddy, but thanks.

"Where's your team?" Cassidy demanded in a low whisper. "You have a team, right? Shouldn't they be here?"

His team was still back at the ballroom, talking with the local authorities and trying to figure out just who those men had been.

For the moment, he and Cassidy were on their own.

Cale quickly considered his options. He could try to get her back upstairs into her room.

And then have the shooter—shooters?—come up after us? Not the best idea.

Or he could get her the hell out of there.

Cale decided to go with option two. His left hand tightened on her. "When I say 'move,' you get into the sports car and you stay low."

She turned her head, meeting his gaze. "You've got keys on you?"

Since it wasn't his car, no, he didn't. But that was just a minor point.

One, two... "Move!" He yanked open the car door. Cassidy jumped inside, staying low, just as he'd told her.

But the shooter saw their movements. He fired, and the glass exploded on the passenger's side of the vehicle.

Cassidy yelled and ducked even lower.

Again—the yells weren't the actions of a trained EOD agent. Civilians yelled. Screamed. Agents went to work.

Cale jumped into the vehicle. He shoved his hands under the dashboard, found the wires he needed—cars had always been a specialty of his—and he had the engine cranking to life instantly.

A good thing because more gunfire was exploding around them.

He shoved the car into Drive and slammed the gas pedal down to the floorboard. They raced from the scene with bullets chasing after them.

His right hand still held the gun, and his left kept a white-knuckled grip around the steering wheel.

"Are you okay?" Cale demanded as they rounded the next corner. The shooter could be pursuing them, so he barely slowed. He was pretty sure the sports car lifted onto two wheels.

She didn't answer him.

"Cassidy!"

She was curled in on herself, crouching down on the floorboard. He could just see the top of her blond head.

"I'm okay." Soft. "I just got cut from some of the glass. No big deal."

He glanced in the rearview mirror. Saw only darkness behind them. But it wasn't like their pursuers would come chasing with their bright lights on.

He wasn't using his lights, either. Because if you wanted to blend in with the darkness, you didn't flash a beacon.

"Are they following us?" Cassidy asked from her crouched position.

Maybe.

The car slid around another corner. He wasn't getting on the main roads, the roads that would still be full of those celebrating Carnival. The party didn't exactly stop just because it was after midnight. He needed to stay away from the party—and the cluster of people that would just slow him down.

He knew this area. This wasn't his first time to visit Rio. The EOD agents had a house not far from their current location. A few miles, a few more backstreets.

Then they'd be safe.

Or as safe as they could be. He needed more intel to figure out what was happening. *Why is she a target?*

Cale didn't like being the hunted. No, it was his job to be the hunter.

And for others to be his prey.

Chapter Three

A long sliver of broken glass protruded from Cassidy's arm. Carefully, she curled her fingers around the glass and pulled it from her skin, hissing out a breath at the pain.

"What are you doing?" She didn't look up at Cale's growl. The guy often seemed to be growling. Not exactly Mr. Sunshine and Light, but then, in her experience, tough guys weren't. They were dark and intense and the ones who were perfect when it came to pulling your butt from the fire.

Hello, fire. Her great escape attempt had almost blown up in her face. If Cale hadn't been there...

It grated, but she needed the agent. She needed the backing of the EOD.

And Cale had sure gotten them out of the shooter's range fast enough.

Hot-wiring the car had been a handy trick, a trick that she'd always wanted to learn. Maybe she could convince him to teach her how to do it. Once they were not being chased by gunmen.

But...for the more pressing matter at hand... "I'm trying to stop the blood flow. That's what I'm doing."

They were in some rundown house on the edge of town. The place had looked abandoned from the outside, and, yes, it pretty much looked that way on the inside, too. Only Cale had told her that it was a safe house.

She wasn't exactly feeling safe. And with 0600 ticking closer and closer, she was running out of time in a hurry.

His fingers curled around her wrist, and he lifted her arm so that he could see the wound. When his face tensed, she realized things were worse than she'd realized. "You need stitches."

Definitely worse. "The blood's stopping."

No, it wasn't.

"There goes that hitch," he said, sounding distracted as he bent to study her wound. "Every time you lie, it's a dead giveaway."

Damn. She would have to be a whole lot more careful. How had she not noticed that slip before? "I don't need stitches." Okay, maybe she did. But, more important, "I don't have time to go to a hospital."

"Forget the hospital. I'll give them to you right here."

Very bad idea. He was kidding, right? She studied his face, met his stare. *Not kidding.* Cassidy quickly shook her head. "Do you even know how many infections I could get from you doing that? No way, I—"

"The wound is deep, and you need stitches. I've got the supplies we need right here."

Because EOD agents were like Boy Scouts.

"Look, if it makes you feel better, I stitched myself back up before I went to your place."

"You...you were hurt?" She hadn't even noticed that. He'd seemed fine as he'd *carried* her out of the party.

"A graze just deep enough to need a couple of stitches." He shrugged it off.

She tried to keep her jaw from dropping. "You get shot a lot, don't you?" How was that normal?

"I try not to."

That wasn't the best answer.

"Come on. We need to get you cleaned up."

He meant stitched up, and though the thought made her queasy, Cassidy sucked in a deep breath and squared her shoulders. It had to be done. So she'd do it.

Then he was leading her into the bathroom. She cleaned away the blood and grime on her. And, yes, the guy did have supplies in that little room. Even latex gloves that he put on right before he got ready to sew her up.

Don't look. Don't look.

"It's going to hurt," he warned her. A second's warning before he started.

She kept her head turned away and bit her lip when she felt the needle slide into her skin. Mercer never would have made a sound. Heck, once the guy had been shot—twice—in the chest. He'd dug the bullets out himself, then taken out the men who'd been after him. Like Cale, he'd stitched himself back up.

Her wound pricked, pulsed.

She could feel every poke of that needle. A little anesthesia would have been awesome.

Her eyes squeezed shut.

This wound was nothing. Mercer had been stabbed four times on a mission in Panama years ago. Those wounds had been so deep, crisscrossing over his chest. She'd been so afraid, then, and—

"I'm done."

Her breath rushed out. She'd made it through. An old trick that she had—just use bad memories to push away the current fear. Fight one fear with another.

It was her way.

Because she knew too much about fear.

Cale finished cleaning up. He put a bandage over her

arm. His fingers seemed to linger against her skin. "Where did you go?" Curiosity had deepened his voice.

Her head turned, and she stared into his eyes.

His jaw locked. His fingers—not covered in latex gloves any longer—rose to her cheeks.

He's wiping away my tears.

She hadn't realized that she'd been crying. Had the tears been due to her wound? Or her memories?

Those stab wounds on Mercer's chest... When she'd seen him in the hospital, looking so broken, she'd been sure that he was dying.

But it would take a whole lot to kill Bruce Mercer.

"You're not an EOD agent," Cale said, sounding absolutely sure.

Her chin jerked up at that. "Don't be so certain. I did a good enough job of saving you back there, didn't I?" He would have taken a bullet to the back if it hadn't been for her. Stitching up her wound hardly made them even.

No matter what he might think.

That steady gaze of his never wavered. "How'd you know the shooter was there?"

"I saw the glint of his weapon." She'd had only an instant to react. She'd shoved Cale with all of her strength.

And saved him.

Point for the debutante.

He stepped away from her—or as far away as the small space would allow. "I want to know your story."

I'm not in the mood to tell it. So she needed to distract him. "Mercer honestly sent you down here without briefing you? I mean, do you usually just unquestioningly follow the guy's every order—"

He'd headed back into what she figured was supposed to be a den of sorts. She followed right on his heels. He spun around, and she had to pull up short so they didn't collide.

After a considering moment, he gave a nod and said, "I'll tell you the mission I was given."

Uh-oh. She didn't like the silky menace in his tone.

"I was told that I needed to head down to Rio and find a party girl named Cassidy Sherridan."

A party girl? Well, that *was* the image she cultivated. *Only that's not the real me.*

"I was directed to follow her every move. To stick to her and make sure she remained safe at all times."

Her brows climbed. Her arm was still throbbing, but she ignored the pain. "That's it? That's all you were told?" Talk about being in the dark. Mercer must have grown even more paranoid about her in recent months.

She'd give Cale a few details since he'd almost gotten shot.

"That's all until I hear from Mercer in—" he glanced at the black watch that circled his wrist "—forty-five minutes."

Not enough time.

She'd have to talk fast. Luckily, she'd always been a fast talker. Cassidy exhaled slowly and began with the truth. "Four years ago, my best friend was abducted from a pub just outside of Dublin." Four years ago, but the memory was just as fresh in her mind. Fear didn't fade. "The men who took her said that she'd be returned if they were paid three million dollars. They got their money, but Helen never came home."

Not alive, anyway. Her body had eventually been found by the authorities.

Helen's death hadn't been fast or easy. No one should die that way.

"Since then, over a dozen other women—wealthy, young, well-connected women like Helen—have been taken. Sometimes…sometimes they are brought back, with only nightmares and shadows as their memories, but other times, their abductors leave their broken bodies behind."

He watched her in silence.

She felt as if she'd just ripped open an old, too-raw wound…because she had. "The leader of the group is a man called the Executioner."

Cale's dark brows rose.

"He named himself—" arrogant, sick jerk "—when he… when he first contacted Helen's father. He said that if he didn't get his money, then Helen would face the Executioner's knife. His knife."

And Helen had faced that knife. The blade had sliced away the beauty of her face before plunging into her heart.

His gaze hardened. "The men at the party…"

"I think they were the Executioner's men." They'd been after their next target. After trying to attract their deadly attention for so long—

Finally, they'd come for Cassidy.

That knowledge was in his eyes. "You set yourself up as bait." Angry, clipped words.

She had. There'd been no choice. "Someone has to stop them!"

His head shook. "The EOD—"

"I'm the one who told the EOD about the Executioner! I'm the one who went to Mercer." Because she'd been so desperate.

"That's why you have him on speed dial."

She waved that away. "My family has connections." As did the families of all the women who'd been taken. "My grandfather is the French ambassador to the U.S. government. Helen's father was an Irish diplomat. The Executioner goes after a certain type of woman—"

"A woman like you." There was fury darkening his words.

"Yes." It made her the perfect bait. The Executioner was

an international killer, and because he hunted in so many places, it was hard for one country—and that country's authorities—to track him.

The faint lines on Cale's face had tightened. "Mercer agreed to let you put yourself up as bait?"

Not exactly. That would be why he kept sending agents to guard her. Only this time, Mercer must have realized just how close she'd finally gotten to the Executioner. "Now that I have the Executioner's attention, I can't walk away. This is my chance."

But Cale's voice roughened even more as he demanded, "Your chance to do what? To wind up dead like your friend?"

Cold, brutal words. She knew his words were supposed to scare her. She'd been dealing with fear too long to let it stop her. "It's my chance to stop him—and his men—before they destroy more lives. If I can get to the Executioner, if I can bring him down…"

"You really think that you're going to do this on your own?"

Her eyes narrowed. Her heart was drumming too fast in her chest. "I've got an EOD agent standing right in front of me. I kind of figured you could do something a little more useful than just being my human shield."

A muscle jerked along the square line of his jaw.

"I mean, what are you?" As Cassidy continued, she let her own anger out. He *would* help her. "The EOD is always ex-military, right? You barely make any sound when you move—your reflexes are the best of any agent I've seen." She could still remember how quickly he'd pulled his gun in that ballroom. "I'm thinking you're—"

"Army ranger. Ex-ranger."

Cassidy nodded. She'd figured as much. "Well, since I conveniently have a former army ranger right here with

me, I thought I might use your services to stop this killer
before he takes any more lives."

Using Cale would sure make things easier on her.

"And what if I hadn't been here?" Cale took a step toward her. "If Mercer hadn't sent me down here to watch
over you—what would you have done then?"

She licked her lips. His gaze fell. Heated. *Oh, boy.*
"Come up with a plan B," she whispered. Actually, she
already had her plan B. It was the plan she'd been using
before she realized who Cale truly was. But plan B involved a whole lot more risk.

His gaze was still on her mouth, and there was a sensual
awareness kindling in his stare. Her heartbeat kicked up
even more, and when had all the air left the room? Sucking in oxygen suddenly became a lot harder.

Her gaze slid over him. Had his shoulders gotten bigger?

"You're in over your head," Cale told her.

He took another step toward her.

That big body of his had been on top of hers when
they'd sought cover on the street. Adrenaline had spiked
her blood, then, and she'd been thinking mainly about
survival, but now...

Now she was thinking far too much about him. "Will
you help me?"

His hands had fisted. Why? So he wouldn't touch her?
She rather liked the feel of his warm, calloused fingertips
on her skin.

"My job is to follow Mercer's orders."

Like a good soldier. Always following orders. "Sometimes, you have to break orders."

His pupils had widened, the darkness swallowing the
blue of his eyes. His gaze was back on her mouth.

He definitely felt the same awareness that she did.

Only he wasn't coming any closer to her.

Fine. She'd get closer to him.

She sucked in another deep gulp of that precious oxygen, and then she was sliding closer to Cale. Her fingers rose and pressed against his chest. He'd ditched the tux and wore a dark T-shirt and jeans. Beneath the thin cotton of the T-shirt, she could easily feel the hard strength of his muscles.

Someone liked to work out. A lot.

"Help me," she said, glancing up at him. "Please, Cale." Then, because it was what she wanted, and she hadn't taken what she wanted in so very long, Cassidy pushed up onto her toes and put her mouth against his.

At first, he didn't move. Not even an inch.

His lips were firm and cool beneath hers, and his body was rock hard. Her mouth moved lightly against his. *Please, don't let this be a mistake. Don't let it be—*

His hands lifted, locked around her and hauled her against him. Their bodies pressed tightly together and his mouth *took* hers.

His lips parted. So did hers. His tongue thrust into her mouth, and, oh, wow, but the agent could sure kiss. Her knees did a little jiggle as she pressed even closer to him.

Heat uncurled in her stomach, a long-denied need that had been buried for too long. But this man, with his strength and the aura of danger that clung to him like a second skin, he made her feel. He made her burn.

He made her want.

Her arm wasn't hurting anymore. Or, if it was, she sure didn't feel the pain. All she could feel was him, surrounding her, making the desire that she felt for him grow ever stronger.

This wasn't about the mission that she'd made her life. This wasn't about avenging a friend.

It was about a man. A woman. Desire.

It was—

His mouth lifted from hers. His fingers bit into her waist. "Did you think it would work?"

Things had seemed to be working just fine here. Her ragged breath indicated things were *more* than fine.

"You aren't going to use your body to make me forget my mission."

Oh, he had *not* just said that to her. Heat burned in her cheeks, and Cassidy knew she had to be flushing a dark red. "That wasn't—"

But his jaw was locked. Desire blazed in his eyes, yet when he spoke, his voice was ice-cold. "I never forget my mission, and I won't be distracted by someone like you."

Someone like you.

The brittle words froze the heat in her cheeks. She'd kissed Cale because she wanted him, but he—he might physically want her, but he sure didn't like that desire.

No. What he didn't like was *her*.

To him, she was—what had he called her?—a party girl.

In that same emotionless voice, he told her, "Whatever help you *thought* you'd seduce me into giving you—"

"I didn't!" Cassidy denied the charge, the urge to scream incredibly strong.

"It's not going to happen." There was a definite arctic chill in his voice.

She straightened her shoulders, grabbing for her pride. "I didn't kiss you because I was trying to manipulate you."

His one raised eyebrow called the words a lie.

"I kissed you because I stupidly wanted you. Don't worry. I won't be making that mistake again."

The door opened behind them. No knock, it just shoved open. Cassidy spun around and saw two big, rather scary-looking men filling the doorway.

The man in front, the guy with the dark hair and the piercing eyes, inclined his head toward her. "Ms. Sherridan."

Of course he knew her, and since Cale wasn't grabbing for a weapon, she figured these two had to be the good guys.

Semi-good, anyway. As good as EOD agents could be.

She realized, too late, that she'd instinctively backed up when her shoulders brushed against Cale. She jerked at the contact, and the man with the eyes that she swore could see right through her—he noted that move.

Wonderful.

The other fellow behind him—talk about intimidating. And she'd thought Cale was dangerous looking? This guy took dangerous to a whole new level. His face wasn't handsome; it was just hard edges, rough lines. His skin was a dark gold, his hair black and his eyes a shining green. He kicked the door shut, secured the lock, then announced, "We've got a problem."

She forced a mocking laugh. "If you call men shooting at us a problem…"

"What's happening, Gunner?" Cale demanded.

Wait, there was a problem *other* than the shooting?

The man he'd called Gunner—Mr. Tall, Dark and Scary—let his bright gaze sweep back to Cassidy. "Your friend, the redhead from the party…"

Her gut clenched. "Genevieve?" Genevieve Chevalier was one of the few people that she actually did count as a friend. She'd known Genevieve since their boarding school days.

Gunner nodded curtly. "She's missing."

Cassidy shook her own head in denial. Genevieve was fine. She'd taken her friend back to Genevieve's hotel after they'd been cleared by the Rio authorities.

"The local cops said they had a guard on her. We thought she was safe." This came from the other guy—the man who was now stalking around the small confines of the room. "We were wrong. When I did a surveillance sweep by her place a little while ago, she was gone and the guard was dead."

Genevieve's gone? If she was and if her guard had been killed, then… "They took her." Dark, twisting fear spread inside Cassidy. If they didn't find Genevieve, fast, then she could be dead.

Tortured, just like Helen.

"We think they came for you," the man began.

"Logan…" A warning note had entered Cale's voice.

This man—Logan—ignored the warning as he kept his focus on Cassidy. "Cale got you away from them, but Genevieve's guard wasn't able to save her. They took her." His lips tightened. "And I want to know *why*."

Another EOD agent who hadn't been briefed. Wasn't Mercer just keeping them all in the dark these days? But she knew why.

Because he doesn't want them to know about me.

Mercer never wanted anyone to know the full truth. Not unless it was absolutely necessary. Because of that secrecy, he'd sent these agents out hunting, blind.

But come 0600, they wouldn't be so blind any longer.

"THE LOCAL COPS have no leads on Genevieve Chevalier's abduction," Logan Quinn said, shoving a frustrated hand through his hair. "With Carnival taking over the city, they are too short-staffed and in way over their heads to handle this case."

A case that was the work of a professional killer and his crew. "You ever hear of a guy called the Executioner?"

Cale asked him, cocking his head as he waited for Logan's response.

Logan was their team leader, the guy who'd earned the moniker of Alpha One in the field. If anyone had intel on the Executioner, it should be him.

And, sure enough, Logan stiffened. "The Executioner? Hell, it fits." Disgust thickened his voice. "He goes after the society princesses—takes them, ransoms them and, half the time, he kills them for sport."

That wasn't exactly what Cale had wanted to hear. He and Logan had headed into the back room while Gunner Ortez, the team's very deadly ex-SEAL sniper, stayed in the den area to keep tabs on Cassidy.

"I guess this mission just became about hostage rescue," Cale said as he turned away from Logan to glance quickly toward the den. Good thing the EOD agents specialized in that area. Even before he'd joined the EOD, Cale had worked plenty of rescue cases on his own. He'd slipped in and out of more hellholes than he could count, rescuing folks that others had given up for dead.

Logan didn't speak.

Cale glanced back at him. "The locals can't handle this. We can." Heading in and out of the dangerous spots that most would never dream of entering and saving those who *couldn't* be saved was their area of expertise.

Cale's phone rang just as Logan opened his mouth to speak. He glanced down, realizing the time. 0600. Mercer was always punctual. He answered the call immediately. "Cale—"

"Is Cassidy in the room?" Mercer's rough voice barked without bothering with any niceties. That was Mercer's way, always cutting through the bull.

"No," Cale said. "But Logan is." He figured Mercer would want to brief him, too.

He figured right.

"Put me on speaker."

Done.

"I know Genevieve Chevalier was taken a few hours ago," Mercer announced. He would. Did anything happen that the EOD director wasn't aware of? "But tell me," Mercer continued, voice even harder, "that Cassidy doesn't know about her abduction yet."

An odd thing to say. "Cassidy knows."

Mercer swore. "She is *not* to go after Genevieve, understand?"

"But as an EOD agent, she can—" Logan began.

"Cassidy isn't an EOD agent. She's an asset, one that I want brought back into the office immediately."

An asset. The lingo used to describe a person who had intel that was often vital to the EOD's success.

Logan stepped closer as he frowned down at Cale's phone. "What about Chevalier? Cale thinks the Executioner may be at work here, and I have to agree with him. Genevieve's abduction sure seems to fit the victim profile developed for that killer."

"Cale's been talking to Cassidy." A new note had entered Mercer's voice. One that Cale couldn't quite understand. "Be careful with her, Cale. Before you know it, Cassidy will have manipulated you into doing anything that *she* wants. I've seen it happen before, with plenty of other agents."

Those words caused tension to harden Cale's muscles. But he'd already known that Cassidy was a manipulator, hadn't he? The instant Cassidy came toward him with her eyes lit with desire, when she put those silken lips against his and so softly whispered...

Help me.

His body had responded instantly to her. How could

he not respond to that sensual invitation? But he'd suspected—damn it—that she was just trying to use him.

Use his desire for her to get exactly what she wanted.

"Cassidy Sherridan is to be brought back to the D.C. office right away." Now there was *no* emotion in Mercer's voice. Just a cold demand. "Cale, you bring her back, got it? I'll send a separate team down to hunt the Executioner—"

"But we're already here, sir," Logan cut in, his frown deepening. "Even if Cale leaves with the woman, Gunner and I can do recon work. We can find this bastard. We can save Chevalier."

"I want you watching Cale's back," was Mercer's fast response. "Guard them every second that Cale and Cassidy are down there. I know those SOBs already made a grab for Cassidy once, and I won't have her falling into their hands. Cassidy's safety *is* the priority. She's to be brought back to the U.S. Once I know she's safe, then I'll make sure that the Executioner is handled."

Cale didn't like this plan. Not when a woman's life was in the balance. "We don't know how much time Chevalier has," Cale snapped, unable to hold back his anger. Just letting a woman stay in a killer's hands? No. That wasn't the way he worked. "We're here, we can—"

"Another team is already en route. And the Executioner… I *know* how he works," Mercer muttered. "He'll be leaving the country ASAP."

All the more reason for them to hunt him, then.

"Get Cassidy back here, Cale, and that's an order." There was a whip of command in the words. "Cassidy *is* the mission. Bring her back. Stay with her, and get her back to D.C. in one piece."

So much for the full briefing that he'd wanted.

Bodyguard duty was continuing, and Genevieve Che-valier—she was just going to be left on her own?

He ended the call and fought to calm the fury that was growing in him. He hadn't agreed to join the EOD so he could stand back while a woman was tortured and killed.

"Cale…you heard the director." Logan was studying him worriedly.

Yes, he'd heard the director.

Jaw locking, Cale gritted his teeth. "Are we just going to leave Genevieve here?"

Cassidy wouldn't want that. He already knew just what kind of fight he'd have on his hands as soon as he tried to force her from Rio.

His gaze guarded, Logan said, "We follow orders."

Right. That was what good soldiers did.

Only…they weren't still in the military.

A plan began to form in his head. Protecting Cassidy was Mercer's stated priority. And as he protected Cassidy, both Logan and Gunner were supposed to have his back.

So where Cassidy went…

We all go.

A grim smile pulled at his lips. Maybe Cassidy would get the help she wanted from him, after all.

And she didn't even have to seduce him in order to get it.

Huh. That was a pity.

When Cale came out of the back room he had a backpack thrown over his shoulder. Cassidy noted the bulge of his weapon under his arm.

She jumped to her feet. "You talked to Mercer." *Genevieve is gone. It's happening again. I have to help her!*

A curt nod from Cale. "It looks like you've got yourself an escort back to the U.S."

"No."

"Yes."

She hadn't even realized the denial had come from her until she heard his clipped response. "We can't leave! We have to help Genevieve!"

"A ransom demand hasn't been given to her family yet," Logan said. Cassidy thought she saw a flash of sympathy in his eyes, but that flash vanished too quickly for her to be certain.

"How do you know that they haven't made contact?" Cassidy fired back, desperate. "They could have—"

"The EOD knows. Mercer assured us that he's keeping tabs on the situation."

"No, he's keeping tabs on me." There was plenty of bitterness in her voice.

"Because you're an asset?" Cale had taken a few more steps toward her.

Cassidy flinched. "Is that what I am?" It figured that Mercer had pulled the old asset card. He'd used that before. Her trick of blending truth and lies? She'd learned it from him. Learned it before she'd even learned how to drive a car.

Some lessons were taught early, and you never forgot them.

"According to Mercer—" it was Logan talking again—the other agent, Gunner, hadn't spoken to her at all while the others had been gone "—you're an important asset that has to be escorted back to D.C., pronto."

This couldn't be happening. One of that bunch had to be sane. "You're all going to escort me away while Genevieve dies? While she's tortured?" If they wouldn't help her, she'd have to help herself—and Genevieve. "Look, those guys—the Executioner's men—they want me. They came to that ballroom looking for me." Cale had been right there when they'd shouted her name.

"What they wanted was to kill you hours ago. That was a bullet that came your way in the alley," Cale said, his hand tightening on the strap of his pack. "Not an abduction attempt."

The guy was missing the obvious. She gave a little growl of her own as she tried to explain what he should know. "They tried to kill *you*, not me. I *saved* your hide, cowboy." And she still hadn't received any gratitude for that.

Logan slanted what could have been an amused glance Cale's way.

"Cowboy?"

What? Now Gunner speaks?

She ignored him and focused completely on Cale. "I saved you, so now you owe me. Help me find Genevieve— or at least, just, please, give me my own fighting chance to save her." *Get out of my way and let me help my friend.*

But he wasn't showing any signs of giving in to her. "I have my orders."

Her shoulders slumped. Cale was just like the others. A robot, following all of Mercer's commands without question. Even if it meant that an innocent woman died.

Cassidy wasn't like that. She wasn't a robot, and she didn't care how angry Mercer became. After all, what was he going to do to her? Send his agents to control her life? Keep her locked up? Secluded?

Been there, done that. Over and over again.

The other agents weren't helping her. Cale wasn't helping. So it was up to her to get the job done.

Maybe the fact that they were all underestimating her… Maybe that would be her trump card. She just had to wait for the perfect moment….

Cassidy let her shoulders sag a little more as if she truly were defeated. "When do we leave?" Her voice came out soft, sad. She was being careful not to let that telling hitch—as Cale called it—slip out.

"Now."

What? She'd sure have to act fast.

"We'll head to the airport right now," Cale continued in his getting-it-done voice. She decided she hated that voice as he added, "You'll be back in D.C. by nightfall."

Her thoughts raced. "I don't have my passport. We'll have to go back to my room and get it."

The Executioner's men might still be watching her hotel. *They'd better be watching.*

Because she needed them to find her.

And take her.

Chapter Four

She had to hurt Cale in order for her escape to work. She didn't want to hurt him, but there was no choice. Sometimes, you had to play dirty in this world.

The SUV—Cale's ride, which had been waiting outside the safe house—pulled to a stop near the side of her hotel. Not the main entrance, because they didn't exactly want the valet staff there advertising their presence, but the staff entrance. A quick in-and-out trip. The other two EOD agents were about twenty feet behind them, waiting across the street. Watching them carefully.

Cassidy's fingers flattened against her jean-clad thighs. "Are you sure I can't change your mind?" She had to try one more time.

Cale turned off the engine and gave a slow shake of his head.

Her breath expelled in a rush. *Right.* Just what she'd thought.

I'm sorry, Cale. And she was. Hurting people wasn't her normal style.

Then Cale was exiting the vehicle and coming around to her side so very quickly. When she climbed out, he kept his body close to hers, shadowing her every step.

Protecting her.

While she prepared to hurt him.

Cale had never searched her. He probably should have done that. If he'd searched her when he'd first found her in that alley, he would have found the small knife that she'd strapped to her ankle.

She stumbled against him, bending low. His arms curled around her sides as he steadied her.

She grabbed for the knife, moving as fast as she could. When she straightened, Cassidy had that knife at his side. "I'm sorry," she whispered.

His eyes—that unforgettable blue—held hers as his body seemed to turn to stone. "You shouldn't do this."

She didn't want to do this to him. "I don't have a choice." They were so close, probably appearing like embracing lovers to any who might glance their way. But one lover wouldn't threaten another with a knife. "You're going to let me go."

He shook his head.

Fine. That had been the response that she had anticipated. And the knife—well, that had just been a distraction...

Because Cale was moving even now with a ripple of motion, an attack designed to knock away the knife.

Again, just what I expected.

But the knife wasn't the threat. She struck out with her left hand—her dominant hand—and caught him in the jaw.

She really did have a good left hook.

He stumbled back, slipped on the broken pavement and fell hard.

And Cassidy didn't stay around to see what would happen next.

Genevieve needed her. Cassidy spun away from Cale and ran for the mouth of the alley that waited just a few feet away.

She heard car doors open. Then slam. She knew that sound meant that the other agents would be coming after her.

Hurry, hurry... She had to get away from the EOD agents.

There wasn't any time to lose. She had a lead of only seconds. But it just might be long enough.

If the Executioner's men were watching...if they saw her... *Come and get me.*

Because this was her last chance to save Genevieve.

CALE SMILED AS he rubbed his jaw. She'd landed a good punch. Not hard enough to take him down, well, not unless he'd wanted to go down.

And he had. The scene had to look believable, after all.

Logan and Gunner's footsteps thundered toward him.

"She did it," Logan sounded a bit impressed. "I wasn't sure that she'd really carry through, but that woman wasn't giving up."

Cale had to admit that part of him was impressed with Cassidy, too.

"Now let's stick to the plan," Cale said to the men. The plan that Cale had made up back at the safe house right before he'd gone out and given Cassidy the news about her imminent departure from Rio. "You two keep your eyes on us, and if you lose visual at any time..."

Logan nodded. "We know exactly what to do."

A risky plan, but it was all that Cale had to work with on short notice.

He rose to his feet and took off running toward the alley. He could only allow Cassidy a few moments' head start. Otherwise, the watchers might realize they were walking into a trap.

A trap that used Cassidy as the bait.

Maybe he should have told her his plan, but he didn't

trust her. Didn't know her well enough to trust her. So he'd done exactly what he had to do.

Cassidy wanted her friend back alive. He wanted to stop a killer.

He turned the corner, running faster now. He saw Cassidy up ahead, trying to scale a chain-link fence. The lady was doing a good job of shimmying up. She'd just reached the top when he caught her ankle.

"Going somewhere?" Cale demanded, making sure the words carried a bite.

Cassidy didn't yell. Didn't scream. She did kick him, a sharp hit that surprised him enough to let her go.

Then the woman heaved herself right over the fence and took off running.

Hell, she was better than he'd thought.

He leaped over the fence. Ran forward—and collided with the Carnival crowd that was already spilling into the street. So what if it was early? During these days in Rio, Cale knew that the party could be on the streets anytime. Music, voices, madness—everywhere.

Cassidy had probably been planning on the crowd. She probably thought it would help her to disappear.

She'd thought wrong.

He kept constant sight of her, moving quickly, shoving people out of his way every few feet.

Then Cassidy turned into another alley.

He was right behind her.

Only this alley didn't have a chain-link fence that she could scale. A brick wall sealed her in.

"No more running," he told her, making sure his voice carried over the roar from the crowd.

Cassidy spun around to face him. "You're wrong. There's always more running. There's—" She broke off, her eyes widening as she looked at something—someone?—behind Cale. He knew what those wide eyes meant.

HIS PREY WAS finally taking the bait. Cale had wondered how long he would have to chase Cassidy up and down those streets before they attracted the right attention.

He whirled around and saw the men coming toward him. Two men and a black van had just sealed off the alley's entrance.

They'd tried to take a shot at him before, so they could be planning to kill him, *then* take Cassidy.

Killing him wasn't an option. He had to stay alive and stay with her.

Taking Cassidy? Yeah, that kind of *had* to happen.

"Don't!" Cassidy immediately yelled as she rushed forward. "Don't hurt him! I'll come with you—just let him go!"

Trying to protect him? *Interesting.* Not that he needed that protection.

The men were wearing black ski masks again. They had guns in their hands.

One ground out, "Boss wants him, too..."

Ah, now *that* was news.

Cassidy tried to push in front of Cale. He pushed her right back behind him. The men needed a warning. "If you hurt her, in any way, I'll make sure you regret it." That was really more of a promise than a warning.

He could disarm the men. Easy enough. But...would he then be able to turn the men against their boss? Be able to get them to give him Genevieve's whereabouts?

Cale wasn't sure. In cases like this, some men never turned on their bosses. Death was an easier route than betrayal for them—and for the families that they would leave behind.

If this was their chance to take down the Executioner, then they had to be taken *inside* the killer's lair.

The men laughed at Cale's words. "You don't get to give the orders." The guy on the right pointed his gun at Cale's head. "You aren't the hero."

He also wasn't the victim. But he could play one, for now.

When the masked men told him to, Cale climbed into the van. He stayed right next to Cassidy. After all, that had been Mercer's order—stay close to her. Every moment.

He'd take down the Executioner *and* he'd do his job.

The Shadow Agents didn't let innocents die, and he wasn't about to let the killer escape from Rio.

The van's side door slammed closed.

And they sped away.

LOGAN QUINN WATCHED the black van race down the narrow road. The men had taken the bait. Now...

He pulled out behind the van, making sure not to tail too closely. After all, he didn't want to spook their prey.

He and Gunner were backup for Cale, so that meant they'd follow him...any place that he went.

"Is the tracking device working?" Logan asked as he slanted a fast glance toward Gunner.

Gunner had a laptop open in front of him. The beacon was flashing on the screen. "Working like a dream. You know Sydney would never send us any equipment that was less than perfect."

No, she wouldn't. Sydney would never risk the lives of any of the Shadow Agents.

Every EOD agent had a small chip implanted just beneath the skin, a precaution that Mercer had insisted on after a particularly brutal mission in which they'd lost an operative.

As long as that chip was in place, they'd be able to track Cale.

Tracking Cale meant tracking the Executioner.

Like Cale, Logan was more than ready to take the man down.

THEY WERE TOSSED into a dark room, a basement holding room that was about twelve feet long and ten feet wide. The gunmen locked them in with only a small lantern left for light.

Locked them inside and walked away.

Cassidy stood completely still in the weak light of the lantern. "I didn't mean for you to get taken with me." Guilt whispered through her words.

Her back was to him. Cale wanted her to face him. "But you did mean to get taken yourself."

"Yes."

Now they were locked up, their weapons had been taken and… "What do you think will happen next? Are you going to disarm the men who come back for us? Going to take them out and make them lead you to their boss?"

Actually, that was his plan, but Cale was curious as to what Cassidy had in mind.

She glanced over her shoulder at him. "I planned to trade my life for Genevieve's."

He laughed, then realized the woman was dead serious. *Bad plan, Cassidy. Bad.*

He stalked toward her, anger making his muscles clench. "That's not happening."

She spun to fully face him. "I'm not letting her die. I have…value that the Executioner doesn't realize. I can make this work."

"Because you're an asset?" An EOD asset. Just what intel did she possess? Others had tried to take down the

EOD before—those who'd been clever enough to discover the division's existence. Agents had been targeted, killed, but the EOD had still come out on top in the end.

No one had destroyed them.

Yet.

"Yes. I have value because I'm an asset."

And she thought to betray the agents. Men and women who were his friends. "I won't let you compromise the EOD."

Her hands had fisted at her sides. "Maybe there are things that are more important than the EOD!"

His fingers curled around her arms, but he made sure not to touch her bandage. He didn't want to hurt her. Shake her, maybe, for the risks that she seemed so willing to take, but not hurt the woman. "Do you have any idea how many agents are undercover right now? If you compromised their work, they'd die. Do you want that on you? All those deaths...*on you?*"

She blinked away what he was pretty sure were tears. "I don't want any deaths on me. That's why I'm here." Then she shoved against him. He kept forgetting how deceptively strong she was. "And why *you* shouldn't be here! This is—"

The basement door opened. Light spilled inside, falling down the narrow staircase.

Cale instantly grabbed Cassidy and pushed her behind him. He couldn't see the face of the man waiting at the top of those stairs.

But it was all too easy to see the gun in his hand.

"Cassidy Sherridan..." That voice—it was the guy from the ballroom. The boss? Or one of his flunkies? "So good to finally have you here."

"Where's Genevieve?" Cassidy called out. "Have you hurt her?"

The man didn't move down the steps.

So Cale started moving toward him.

"I've only hurt her a little," the man said. "Not too much—I still have to give proof of life. Can't do that if she's bleeding all over the place. Families doubt when there's too much blood."

Cale was at the bottom of the steps.

Logan and Gunner would have followed him to this location. They were probably outside, trying to figure out the best way to storm inside and take over. Cale just needed to buy them time.

"You've made a big mistake," Cale told the man.

"No." The gun lifted, pointed right at Cale's chest. "You have. You should have left the girl alone. Just let her come to me in that ballroom. It would have saved you a world of pain if you'd stepped aside."

He was going to fire. Cale knew it, and he moved in an instant, lunging to the right even as the bullet blasted out of the man's gun.

Cale just didn't move fast enough.

The bullet thudded into him. He jerked back, twisting, and fell onto the dirty floor.

Cassidy rushed toward him, and her fingers flew over his body. "Cale!"

"Don't worry, I wasn't shooting to kill. That was a warning, Ms. Sherridan. You see, I'm not playing games. I will destroy anyone who gets in my way. And next time… unless you do exactly what I say…the bullet will kill your lover."

The door squeaked as it closed. Then the heavy bolt was thrown into place once more.

"Cale?" Cassidy's voice was broken. Carefully, slowly, she rolled him over. "Please, Cale, tell me that—"

He opened his eyes. "I'm fine." He caught her hands.

"The bullet barely grazed me." Because he'd moved quickly.

"But—but I heard it hit you."

So he was lying. The bullet was in his side, burning him, and he was bleeding a little more than he'd like, but the wound wouldn't kill him. He'd had much worse. "I'm fine," he said again.

She was on her knees beside him. "I didn't want you hurt."

His blood wasn't on her hands. "I chose to go after you."

"You were following orders." Her trembling fingers slid down his cheek.

He caught her fingers. Rose up toward her and ignored the pain. Their captors thought he was weak now. A mistake on their part. "We're getting out of here, and we're getting your friend out." Because that guy had confirmed that he had Genevieve. It was doubtful that he had two separate prison locations for his victims. So Genevieve was probably somewhere in the building. They just had to find her.

He realized that his mouth was just inches from Cassidy's. She hadn't backed away when he'd risen. Her fingers curled around his shoulders. "You knew all this would happen, didn't you?" There was a new understanding in her voice.

"You mean following you after you decked me…that it would lead us to the missing woman? To the killer?"

He heard the faint click of her swallow. "My hit didn't knock you down, did it? It didn't take you out any more than that bullet did."

He smiled and wondered just how much she could see in that weak light. "I was always a pretty good actor."

The sound she made was half laugh, half sob. Then her arms were tightening around him. "Thank you!"

Because he'd gone against orders?

Or "bent" those orders?

For her.

Her mouth was too close. She was too tempting, and the knife edge of adrenaline and fury weakened his control just enough that he had to—

Take.

His lips closed over hers. Not easy. Not soft. He thrust his tongue into her mouth and savored her taste. Cassidy's taste—it was so sweet and hot. When he kissed her, he craved things that he shouldn't.

He forgot the mission.

Forgot protocol.

Wanted.

Her. Naked. Beneath him, in bed.

And I will have her that way.

"So I guess your seduction worked," he murmured against her lips.

He felt the ripple of surprise that trembled through her. She pulled her head back, shook it slightly. "I wasn't…"

"When we're out of here, you'll owe me." A sensual promise. He'd make sure she paid exactly what was owed.

Cassidy didn't speak.

Cale forced himself to let her go. Their captors would be coming back soon. They needed to be ready. "Look for a weapon." Something small they could use against their enemies. They just needed the element of surprise on their side.

They'd get it, especially with Gunner and Logan working nearby.

She eased away from him and began searching with the lantern's light. "There's nothing here."

No, not a damn thing. Except…the lantern.

The bolt slid free upstairs. The door began to squeak open. He took the lantern from her.

The door opened more, spilling light.

Cale lifted the lantern. He waited just a few more precious seconds. Then he threw down the lantern, shattering it. Even as a voice swore at the top of the stairs, Cale was picking up a chunk of broken glass. Not the knife he liked to use, but it would get the job done.

Because when it came to close-contact warfare, he was the best.

The men wouldn't have a target down there now. There wasn't enough light to see. They couldn't shoot from above.

He wrapped his left hand around Cassidy's arm, pulled her back.

Then he smiled up at the silhouette that waited on that staircase.

Come and get me.

"WHAT THE HELL do you mean?" Mercer roared into the phone. "She's taken? Cassidy? Damn it, Logan, I gave your team an order. Cassidy was to be watched, protected at all costs!" The EOD director's furious voice blasted in Logan's ear.

Logan kept his own voice calm as he replied, "She's not alone, sir. Cale is with her."

That didn't seem to reassure him. "He better make sure that she's not so much as bruised. Do you hear me?"

Actually, Logan was hearing a whole lot of emotion in the director's voice—emotion that had never been there before, and he'd worked on plenty of cases with Mercer during his time at the EOD.

"Cassidy *is* the priority. She is the mission." Mercer sounded like the words were being torn from him. "You do *whatever* is necessary to get her out alive. Do you understand? There are no restrictions on this case. If the enemy gets in your way, you take them out. All of them."

Mercer's words were too ragged. There was too much fury—and fear—in his orders.

This wasn't just about some asset.

What are we involved in? What is Cassidy to him?

The director had always told him that cases weren't supposed to get personal, but right now Mercer was crossing all the lines that he'd drawn himself.

"If anything happens to Cassidy Sherridan, I will destroy your team."

Logan stiffened at that guttural vow. "Don't threaten me." He didn't care who he was talking to.

"Then don't screw up! You had an order—bring her in. You think I don't know what this is? Your team is too good to let this happen unless you *wanted* it to happen."

Logan didn't reply. His gaze was on the darkened building that waited less than a hundred feet away. The building that he'd soon be storming.

"You wanted to take out the Executioner, didn't you? And you thought you'd use my—use Cassidy to do it." The slipup had been brief, but Logan had heard it. "When Cassidy is back, there's going to be a full accounting. Do you hear me? Your whole team will be up for review with me. Now do your job—*get her out of there.*" Mercer swore. "I'm sending the others who've been on standby. I *won't* risk her."

The line went dead.

The others?

Mercer has more agents down here. They've been watching us. So that meant that backup would be coming their way. Even if those agents didn't have eyes on them, Mercer could track Logan—the same way that Logan and Gunner had tracked Cale.

Logan shoved his phone aside, picked up his weapon and got ready for the battle that was waiting.

SHE HADN'T PLANNED to pull Cale into this mess. He wasn't supposed to be a hostage.

If anything happened to him because of her, Cassidy knew she'd feel the aching guilt every day for the rest of her life.

No, Cale is strong. He's probably been in and out of every hellhole on earth.

But he'd been shot moments before. He was weak. He couldn't handle these men while he was hurt.

Despite what he might think, the man was only human.

"Stay behind me." Cale's words were the barest whisper.

He had a weapon, of sorts, clutched in his hand. A broken shard of glass. She'd grabbed a chunk of the glass, too. She wasn't going to be dcfenseless, no matter what was coming her way.

She should have told Cale the full truth about herself—that there had been no need for him to be captured.

Not when the cavalry always had a direct linkup to her…and her location.

She'd had a plan in place. The minute she'd vanished from Cale's sight, Mercer should have been alerted.

Her hand rose to her shoulder. The smallest spot of raised flesh was there, hiding her tracking device. Mercer had made sure she had the device implanted. When she'd vanished, he would have been notified immediately. He would have gotten a GPS lock on her—he would have sent in his men….

And then the Executioner could have been taken down.

The plan had seemed so perfect, mostly because the only threat had been to her.

But now Cale was a hostage with her. He was wounded, and he was about to launch himself at the men coming down the stairs.

Four men were rushing toward them. Cale just had that broken glass. He couldn't defeat them all.

He doesn't have to defeat them. Mercer will have learned about my abduction by now—the other agents who'd worked with Cale would have reported to him. So Mercer had probably already started tracking her.

Cale didn't have to risk his life.

All they had to do was keep their captors distracted.

I have to keep Cale alive.

Because while the Executioner might be planning to use her, Cale would be disposable to him.

And if Cale came out of that darkness fighting...

His body was tense. Ready to spring out and attack.

Cassidy couldn't let him do it. She couldn't let him risk himself that way.

She ran away from him, racing toward the stairs.

"Cassidy!" Cale shouted.

But he hadn't been prepared for her move. So he couldn't stop her.

She nearly collided with a man in a black ski mask.

His hands flew out and locked around her.

The chunk of glass fell from her fingers. "Please don't hurt him!"

The man's fingers tightened around her, and he yanked her against him, spinning her so that her back pressed against his chest. "Why ever not?" His voice was deep, rumbling, terrifying. "I enjoy hurting people."

But the Executioner had never taken a man hostage. In all the time that she'd been following him, he'd never picked a male for his prey.

Until now.

"It was a mistake. You wanted me, not him." Her breath was ragged, and the trembling in her voice wasn't an act. The fear was real. "You've got me. Let him go."

Cale had lunged forward. He waited now, at the foot of the stairs, his hands clenched into fists. The light from the top of the stairs barely illuminated him.

"I'm not letting him go. Your hero nearly ruined everything for me." Her captor's breath blew over her ear. "So I'm going to make sure he suffers."

"No!" Cale suffering *wasn't* part of the plan. "You have me—let him go!"

"Get him," the man said to the others as he climbed back up the stairs, pulling Cassidy with him.

The bodies of the other men shoved against her as they ran for Cale.

"No!" Cassidy yelled.

Only…

There was the thud of fists connecting with flesh. Three men had closed in on Cale. Three against one.

One of the Executioner's guards fell down, groaning. A second joined him moments later.

Cassidy saw the flash of Cale's weapon as he sliced out at the third attacker.

Vicious. Fast. Deadly. The fight happened in a matter of seconds, and all three of Cale's attackers wound up on the floor, groaning and immobile.

"Now I'm coming for you," Cale said as he started to make his way up the stairs. "So you need to get your hands *off* her."

But her captor's hands had tightened, and Cassidy felt the sharp slice of a blade on her neck.

"Can you see the knife in my right hand?" the man holding her demanded. "Because it's at her throat. You take one more step, *hero,* and I'll slice her from ear to ear."

Cassidy wasn't breathing.

She knew the man meant exactly what he said.

Cale stopped advancing. "You're bluffing. If she's dead, then you can't use her. You can't ransom her."

"No, but there are others like her. Rich, useless women who can be taken and controlled. There are always more, just waiting to be taken."

Waiting to be killed?

She heard the thud of footsteps behind them. More of the Executioner's men, coming to help him.

Coming to hurt Cale? To kill him?

How much more time needed to pass before help came for her and Cale?

Cassidy licked her lips. "Was…Helen McDonough… so useless? So easy to control?"

She felt his start of surprise against her.

Cale advanced a step.

"Helen?" the man repeated. "I remember her so well. She was my first. You never forget your first."

She wanted to sink that knife into *his* throat. "She was my friend!"

Cale crept up another step.

"She was a spoiled princess who begged while I sliced her…. *Begged…*" He jerked Cassidy back, yanking her up the stairs and away from Cale. They crossed the threshold and stumbled into another room. "Just like you'll beg before I'm done with you."

Chapter Five

And, with his cold, brutal words, Cassidy let the mask that she'd worn for so long fall away. Her fear was real—but so was her rage.

"No. I won't beg." She shoved back with her elbow as hard as she could. He grunted, and his hold loosened. That little bit of slack was all she needed. Cassidy ducked, dropping right from under his arm. The knife sliced over her, but she didn't care.

"Cassidy!" Cale's bellow. His footsteps thundered up the stairs.

She swiped out with her hand and yanked the ski mask off the man who'd held her. The man who spoke of Helen's death so callously.

The Executioner.

His men were crowding in behind him. Some held guns. Some had no weapons at all.

She ignored them.

Hurry, Mercer, hurry.

Cassidy stared up at the monster who'd haunted so many of her dreams. Only he didn't look like a monster.

Under the bright light, his blond hair gleamed. His face was handsome, cut in smooth, clean lines. He could have been any man that she'd met at a dozen parties.

He should have looked as evil as he was.

He offered her a smile. "Not what you expected, am I?" He lifted his knife, a knife red from her blood. "Don't worry. By the time I'm finished, you'll have changed your mind."

"No!" Cale's voice. He burst from the basement. "You won't be—"

An alarm sounded, then, the shrill cry echoing through the building, and that jarring sound was a relief to Cassidy. The most beautiful sound that she'd ever heard.

If the alarm was sounding, then that meant…

"He was followed!" the Executioner cried. "Damn it, we have to—"

Gunfire exploded. Only the gunfire didn't come from the weapons that the Executioner's men held. The bullets hit the Executioner's men, taking them out.

The Executioner reached for Cassidy, but Cale was there, shoving him back, driving his weapon at the blond man even as the Executioner sliced with his own blade.

The scent of blood deepened.

And the gunshots kept blasting.

The Executioner stumbled back. He stared down at his blood-covered chest in shock. "No, not to me…" He lifted his weapon once more. "You don't stop—"

Bullets slammed into his exposed chest. One hit. Two. Three. He jerked back with each impact, as if he were a puppet being yanked on a string. Blood dripped from his mouth. His eyes went wide, then he fell back, slamming into the floor.

His men—those still alive, anyway—began firing back at their assailants. A bullet blazed just past Cassidy's arm, so close that she felt the burn on her skin.

Then Cale was there, shielding her, rushing her toward the door on the right. He made sure his body covered hers for every step that they took.

He ripped open the door.

Over his shoulder, she saw men coming from the shadows. Men who moved with a lethal precision that marked them as hunters. She counted four—no, five of them.

"Cassidy?"

The voice came from inside the room that she and Cale had just entered. It was weak and scared…and the whispery voice belonged to Genevieve.

Cassidy rushed toward her. Genevieve was tied to a chair. Her friend was sobbing, shaking. She'd nearly managed to break free from her bonds; the rope was barely clinging to her wrists.

Cale cut through the remaining rope with the glass he still held. Just a piece of glass, but it was a weapon he'd used with brutal efficiency time and again.

"What's happening?" Genevieve demanded as she reached for Cassidy. "Those shots…" Tears leaked down her cheeks. "Are we going to die?"

"No." Cale's voice was certain. "I'm getting you both out of here."

She believed him. After the way she'd seen him take down those men—just with that shard of glass—she was ready to believe that Cale could do anything.

The door flew open behind them.

Cale spun, body tensing, as he faced the new threat.

Cassidy recognized the man in the doorway. Logan—Cale's teammate.

"Figured you could use some backup about now." Logan's gaze slid to Cassidy, narrowed. "Apparently Mercer figured the same thing. He sent in a full detail with guns blazing."

She could still hear those blazing guns.

Logan inclined his head when he noticed Genevieve's huddled form. "You saved the girl."

"And stopped the killer," Cassidy said, straightening. The gunfire—it had just ended.

Genevieve's cries deepened behind her.

"The Executioner is dead," Cassidy told Logan.

"He'd be the blond out there," Cale added. "The one with three bullets in his chest and his right shoulder carved open."

"You do like to play rough," Logan muttered.

"The bullets came from someone else. I'm guessing that full detail you mentioned, because I know Gunner would have only needed one shot."

Genevieve grabbed for Cassidy's arm. "Get me out of here!"

Cassidy nodded.

Logan checked behind him. Then he tapped a small, black headset at his ear. "Are we clear?" A pause. "Then I'm bringing them out."

Cale reached for Cassidy's left hand.

Did he stumble?

She studied his face. He was pale, far paler than she'd ever seen him before. "Cale needs help! He was shot."

His fingers tightened on hers. "Baby, I got this."

How could he sound so calm? So…certain?

But then they were being led back out of the room, and Genevieve's cries grew worse at the sight that confronted her.

Blood. Death.

"I don't know how he got these guys here so fast," Logan mused as he surveyed the team that was making quick work of cleaning up the bloody scene. "I figured when I gave him the news that Mercer would track your unit, Cale, but then he already had these men just mere miles out as Gunner and I were getting into launch position."

His unit? Oh, Cale had a tracker, too.

They didn't know about her own device.

Because they didn't know about her.

"Ma'am?"

Cassidy glanced up and saw a man standing before her. He had close-cropped, black hair and golden eyes. A long scar cut across his right cheek. He wore all black, and he had a gun holstered at his side. He offered his hand to her. "You're supposed to come with me, Ms. Sherridan."

Ms. Sherridan? That guy knew her better than that.

Cale immediately shoved that offered hand to the side. "The hell she is, Lancaster."

So Cale knew him, too. Not surprising. Agent Lancaster had been with the EOD for a few years now.

Lancaster slanted his gaze toward Cale. "You'll need that wound tended to."

Cale's body all but vibrated with rage. "What I need is for you—"

"Russell, Owens…you two make sure that Ms. Chevalier is checked out and returned home." Two more men in black moved toward Genevieve at Lancaster's order.

Genevieve inched closer to Cassidy. "What's going on? Who are these men, Cassidy?"

"It's okay." Cassidy gave her a hug. "They're the good guys." *Mostly.* "They'll keep you safe."

After a moment, Genevieve nodded and slowly walked away with the men.

Lancaster still stood in front of Cassidy. "I've got my orders. Mercer wants me to bring her in." He was staring at Cassidy, but his words were for Cale.

"She stays with me. I'm the one who—"

"You're the one who used her so that he could play hero and take down the Executioner." Lancaster's voice was flat. "Mercer knows *exactly* who you are."

No, he had that wrong. Cale hadn't used her. She was the one who'd put him in jeopardy.

"You don't seriously think he just…let you go, do you, Ms. Sherridan?" Lancaster shook his dark head. "Mercer was very clear on what Cale was to do on the extraction… and he didn't follow orders."

"So now you're taking over?" Cale gritted out.

"Yes, I am."

But Cassidy didn't want to go with him. She…she trusted Cale. She wanted to be with him.

So she twined her fingers with his. "Where I go, he goes."

Lancaster's dark brows climbed.

"So unless you have orders to physically pry me away from him—" doubtful, though she wouldn't put that past Mercer "—then you can escort us both out of here. You *aren't* taking me away from Cale."

A muscle jerked in Lancaster's jaw. "Figured you'd be as stubborn as Mercer."

Her breath caught. *He knew.* But then, Lancaster had worked with her longer than most agents had.

A faint smile lifted Lancaster's lips. There were secrets in his eyes. Plenty of them.

Cassidy knew she would have to deal very, very carefully with Agent Lancaster.

MOST FOLKS WOULD have never noticed the small clinic. It wasn't in the heart of Rio, wasn't close to the Carnival celebration. It was near the jungle, barely clinging to the edge of civilization. The doctor there knew how to keep quiet—and he also knew how to hurriedly patch an ex-soldier's wounds.

No anesthesia was given. Cale didn't want anything to dull his senses. The bullet was pulled from him; the stitches sank into his skin. Cassidy stayed by his side every moment, her worried gaze on him.

Blood streaked her clothes. Blood and dirt. She had to be exhausted after all that she'd been through, but the woman remained on her feet, stubbornly holding his hand like it was a lifeline for her.

Or for him.

This…*this* was the spoiled debutante that he'd scoffed at before?

Hell, no. This woman was completely different. She was strong, and brave, and…

He wanted her so badly that he ached. The newest bullet wound he had didn't matter. The bruises and aches in his body were all but forgotten.

Cassidy—and the growing need that he felt for her—consumed him.

He couldn't take his eyes off her face. So lovely. So perfect. When the Executioner had put his knife to her throat, when Cale had thought that Cassidy might die…

I went a little mad.

He'd raced up those stairs and had been ready to beat the man to death in an instant. Been ready to do anything for her.

"Finished." The doctor's English was rough, but his fingers were fast enough as they snapped up the money that Logan offered for services rendered.

"Obrigado." Cale thanked him in Portuguese.

The doctor nodded, then hurried from the small room. Logan followed him.

Cale was left alone with Cassidy.

Finally.

He eased up, feeling the stretch of those new stitches as he sat on the edge of the metal exam table. Cassidy's leg brushed against his.

"Take it easy," she said, eyes worried. "You don't want to undo the man's work so soon."

He pulled her closer, positioning her so that she stood between his spread knees. "You were wearing a mask." He could see that now. No, see *her*.

She blinked at him. "Uh, Cale, did you hit your head at any time during that fight? Maybe it's too much blood loss…."

His fingers rose and curled around her chin. "Stop, Cassidy. I see you now."

For an instant, fear flashed in her eyes, but she blinked and the emotion was gone.

Just like that.

She was very good at wearing her mask.

A much better actor than he was.

"What do you think it is that you see?" Her lips twisted. "A woman who almost got you killed?"

"A woman who was willing to risk her life to stop a killer."

Her lashes lowered. "I didn't want you hurt. You can't keep taking bullets for me."

His hand went to hers once more. He brought her fingers to his bare chest.

She flinched at the contact.

He had to bite back a groan. Her hand was so soft, and she was—caressing him. Almost as if she didn't even realize what she was doing.

Swallowing, he moved her fingers, making sure that she felt all of the scars that marked him. Old bullet wounds. Knife wounds. Too many battles over too many years.

"I'm used to risk," he told her.

Her lips parted as a soft sigh slipped from her. "But this risk should have been mine, not yours."

She was tracing the scar on his left side, just a few inches above his nipple.

His pants were too tight, and Cale knew she had to see his arousal. There was no hiding some things.

But Cassidy didn't back away from him.

She eased even closer.

His heartbeat kicked up.

"I've never seen anyone fight the way you did."

When it came to up-close kills, he knew he had a brutal talent. But that wasn't something he would have chosen for her to see.

I guess we're both seeing things we shouldn't. "Why do you do it?" Cale asked, voice deep and rough because the arousal he felt for her pulsed through him. "Why do you pretend to be the party girl, flitting from one ballroom to another?"

"Maybe that is who I am." Where his voice had been rough, hers was soft. Husky. "No pretending needed."

He didn't buy it anymore. "No. You're the woman who didn't flinch when the Executioner had his knife at her throat." Even though she'd flinched when she'd touched Cale's chest.

So many contradictions.

So much mystery.

That was Cassidy.

"You're strong and you're smart, and you *don't* let fear control you."

Her gaze met his. She didn't stop touching him. "That's because I can't let it control me. I won't."

She was so much stronger than he'd realized. *I was a fool.*

"They're going to try to take me away from you." Cassidy's soft words made him furious—because he knew they were true.

He'd screwed up. He hadn't protected her as he should have, and now Mercer already had other EOD agents there to take over her case.

One agent in particular...

Drew Lancaster. The guy was good—cold but good. Former Delta Force, Lancaster had a reputation for emotionless hunts. Some said he had ice that pumped through his veins, not blood.

"I guess that's the way it works, right? Agents come, agents go." Her smile was bittersweet. "But I'm not going to forget you as easily as I have the others."

"Damn straight, you're not." He sure wouldn't be forgetting her anytime soon, and—he didn't want to let her go.

So he tightened his hold on her.

"Why did you kiss me in that basement?" Cale asked her, unable to hold back the question. She hadn't needed to seduce him then.

"I did it for the same reason that I kissed you the first time."

The first time her lips had brushed against his, Cale had thought that she was trying to manipulate him with sex.

A trick that wouldn't have worked coming from most women.

Only she wasn't most women. He was finding that he would do just about anything for her.

"What was the reason?" he pressed, because he wanted to hear her confession.

"Don't you already know?" Then she leaned toward him. Her lips feathered lightly over his. "Because I want you, Cale Lane. I kissed you the first time because I needed to feel your mouth on mine, and the second time—it was about need, too. About me wanting you, needing you, as a memory to hold against anything bad that could happen to me in that terrible place."

Had she thought that she might not escape the Executioner alive?

Her lips molded to his.

His mouth opened as he took control of the kiss. He wanted more than just a light touch from her. He wanted everything.

That was exactly what he was determined to have.

He'd never get used to her taste, a combination of sweet and rich flavor—like champagne and chocolate. He felt like he could get drunk from her. Touching her, tasting her, made the blood pump harder in his veins. Her breasts pushed against him, the nipples tight peaks, and he wanted to strip away her clothes. To see all of her.

But not in some run-down clinic that was sinking into the jungle. Not with half a dozen agents waiting outside the door.

He wanted her, and he wanted them to be far away from the rest of the world.

That's not happening now.

As if in echo of his thoughts, a knock sounded at the door. Cassidy tried to pull back. He didn't let her go.

The door swung open.

He kept his mouth on hers, because he wasn't done with her.

"That's a really bad idea, Lane," Drew Lancaster said as he entered the room.

From where Cale sat, it was the best idea that he'd had in a long time.

Because he hadn't ever wanted someone as much as he wanted her.

Taking his time, Cale lifted his head. Then he eased from the table, making sure to keep Cassidy close. "You're interrupting, Drew."

Drew shook his head. "I'm just here to tell the lady that

her ride is waiting. Mercer pulled his strings, and our flight leaves in just over an hour."

Mercer was always pulling strings, playing them all.

Drew turned to Cassidy. "He wants you back on U.S. soil."

"Is Cale coming with us? Because I told you—I won't leave without him."

Drew showed no surprise at Cassidy's demand. "Don't worry. He's coming. The director is particularly looking forward to a little chat with him."

Wonderful. He'd just joined the EOD a few months ago, and now he might find himself getting kicked out of the division because he'd refused to follow orders.

Being a team player didn't always work so well for him.

"It's okay," Cassidy said to Cale. "I'll make Mercer understand what happened."

Hard to do. Cale realized that Cassidy didn't fully understand what had happened herself. She thought that she'd duped him, that she'd escaped.

She still didn't get that he'd used her as bait.

What the hell was I thinking?

"Mercer wants you to call him, Ms. Sherridan," Drew said as his attention swept between her and Cale. "You need to check in with him before we leave for the flight."

"Right." She pushed back her shoulders, as if bracing herself. "Better get this over with." Then she was heading for the door.

Cale didn't move. He just watched her walk away—his focus on the slight sway of her hips.

He was drawn to everything about her.

He was in so much trouble.

The door shut behind her with a soft click. As soon as Cassidy was gone, Drew gave a low whistle. "Don't get me wrong, man. I can understand the temptation."

Since when did Agent Ice understand any kind of temptation?

"But you don't seem to get who you are messing around with," Drew continued. "Mercer will crucify you for this."

"I kept Cass—I kept the asset safe," Cale corrected himself deliberately. Mercer might not like his methods, but he'd done his job. "And I brought down an internationally wanted killer. I think Mercer can stand to cut me some slack."

Drew rocked back on his heels. "You need to pay more attention to what's right in front of you."

What the hell was that supposed to mean?

"You need to watch yourself with Cassidy Sherridan." Now it sounded like Drew was giving him a warning. "She's not at all what she appears to be."

He'd already figured that out on his own.

"A woman like her will burn you, and if you aren't careful, there won't be anything left but ash."

Drew turned away.

Cale lunged after him. He grabbed the guy's arm. "How do you know so much about Cassidy?"

"Because I've been on guard duty with her a few times before."

At those words, a stab of jealousy shot through Cale. Jealousy? Why would he be jealous of another agent doing his job?

But…that *job* was Cassidy, and he sure didn't like the idea of Drew Lancaster being so close to her.

"On my last stint with Cassidy, I was on protection detail with her for three months. You can learn a lot about a person when you watch her 24/7."

Cale's back teeth clenched.

"You just met her, didn't you? Known her only a few days…" Drew pulled away from him. "Take the advice that

I'm giving, man. Don't get close to her. Kissing her was probably the worst mistake you could've made."

Cale forced a mocking smile. "Nah, I don't think it even ranks in my top ten."

A furrow appeared between Drew's eyes. "I heard the rumors about you. That you're not even supposed to be in the EOD. That you have—"

"Overly aggressive tendencies?" Cale quoted from what he knew was in an old case file—courtesy of a shrink who'd been out to punish him. "That I'm prone to extreme violence?" He'd sure gotten violent with those jerks in that basement.

Because they'd tried to come between him and Cassidy.

Drew studied him. "At first, I thought the rumors were B.S. Hell, show me a soldier who isn't aggressive."

Aggression was part of who they were.

"But I saw what you left behind in that basement, Hoss." Drew's Mississippi drawl roughened the words. "And now I know exactly how you like to play."

Cale stared back at him. "I wasn't playing."

"Cassidy isn't for you. She's not supposed to wind up with a soldier who likes to kill."

He didn't flinch. Barely.

"There are other plans in place for her. You need to remember that before it's too late."

Then Drew turned his back on Cale and opened the door.

Cale didn't follow him. He was too busy remembering the feel of broken glass in his hands.

He could still smell the blood. Still hear the grunts from the guards.

A soldier who likes to kill...

What chance did he have with a society princess?

He knew they were different, from two worlds that couldn't have been farther apart.

Only… *I want her.*

She was the first thing he'd wanted for himself in longer than he could remember.

And Cale had no plans to walk away from her.

Chapter Six

The looming building that housed the EOD rose before Cassidy. She didn't normally head into the main office because Mercer liked to keep her away from that area.

He'd always said that the fewer people who actually knew about her, the better.

She'd refused to let his words hurt her. No, she'd refused to act like they hurt.

Because they had.

The hustle and bustle of Washington, D.C., zoomed past her. Night had fallen again, and the city seemed to beat with a pulse of life. Tourists strolled on the sidewalks, impatient cabdrivers zipped through the traffic and that big building just waited.

It wasn't like anyone could prance inside and see Elite Operations Division emblazoned on the windows and doors of the offices. The EOD operated below the radar—most civilians would never know of its existence.

Armed guards waited just inside the lobby, and no one got past those guards, not without some very good clearance. So any clueless tourists who wandered inside, looking for a bit of D.C. history, would quickly find themselves escorted elsewhere.

The SUV pulled to a slow stop near the EOD headquarters. Drew turned toward her. He'd been her companion for the past twelve hours. He…and Cale. Cale had been on the plane with her. Cale's two teammates—Logan and the ever-quiet Gunner—had been there, too. Only now, Cale, Logan and Gunner were in the vehicle behind them.

They had all been asked to come to Mercer's office. She knew Mercer must have plans to berate them for her capture, but she wasn't going to let those men be punished. *She'd* left; *she'd* disobeyed his orders. Not them.

"Cassidy…" Drew's sigh of her name had her glancing at him. At least he'd finally dropped the annoying "Ms. Sherridan" bit. When her focus landed on him, he said, "You…you need to be careful with Cale Lane."

She actually liked Drew. Sure, she'd heard the whispers that the guy was supposed to bleed ice water, but she'd never found him particularly cold. He'd talked to her during his guard assignments. He hadn't acted like she was an annoying piece of fluff that he had to deal with—the way most agents usually did. Heck, even the way that Cale had originally looked at her.

I see you now. Cale's words rang through her mind. She couldn't get the man *out* of her mind.

"There have been some rumors about him," Drew continued. "I just… You're not as strong as you think, Cass, and I know just how cosseted Mercer has made sure that you are."

Cosseted… Was that his slang for guarded? Locked up? Kept away from the opposite sex? Because until she'd hit eighteen, she'd been in a boarding school—that was where she'd met Helen and Genevieve. And after she'd finished college, her father had made sure that her guard duty was in place. He'd amped up the protection when Helen had died—and when Cassidy had started her hunt for the Executioner.

"Just because he's an agent, it doesn't mean that you should trust him."

His words floored Cassidy. *You're wrong.* "Mercer trusts him. You know he wouldn't have sent Cale if he didn't believe—"

"Cale *used* you to get the Executioner."

She shook her head. He had it so wrong.

But Drew was adamant. "He let you escape him. Do you really think a guy like Cale would have been caught off guard by a left hook?" Drew shook his head. He knew her signature move so well—mostly because he'd taught it to her. "I've seen him take down half a dozen guards in a matter of seconds. One blow—no matter how power-ful—wouldn't stop him."

And she'd seen Cale go through all those men in that basement, slashing out brutally with that chunk of glass as his only weapon.

"He wanted to stop the Executioner." Her words were soft, but they seemed too loud in the interior of that SUV.

"Yeah, that's what he wanted, but his *job* was to protect you, not to put you in harm's way as he used you as bait."

Drew wasn't understanding. "I used myself as bait."

"He's a trained agent—you're not!" Now the ice that he was so famous for seemed to crack. "He could have gotten you killed. I know his orders because Mercer gave the same ones to me. Get you out. Get you back to D.C. and then—"

"And someone else would come for Genevieve?" Cassidy finished.

Silence.

"She might not have lived long enough for that some-one else to come for her." She shoved back her hair, sud-denly feeling very, very tired. "And the Executioner would have gotten away. Been free to take and kill someone else.

Mercer has had years to stop the guy, but the killer was too good. He slipped away too many times." This had been her best shot at stopping him.

"Be careful with him, Cass," Drew told her, and his eyes looked worried. "Don't let emotions lead you to trust the wrong man."

Then he was climbing from the SUV. Guards had spilled from the interior of the building. Come for her. She exited the vehicle and glanced to the left. Cale was already standing on the sidewalk, waiting.

She didn't see Logan and Gunner. Had they gone inside already?

Time to face Mercer.

Then she was being led inside. Cassidy couldn't help tensing. She was always tense in this place. She'd never felt welcome there, maybe because Mercer had made so sure that she understood...

This part of my life isn't for you.

They climbed into the elevator—just Cassidy, Cale and Drew. When her gaze slid to Cale, she found his stare locked right on her.

She was pretty sure that Drew swore under his breath and muttered, "Mistake."

But wasn't it her mistake to make?

The nightmare that she'd lived with for years was over—the monster, dead. Why couldn't she celebrate? Wasn't she entitled to a little bit of happiness?

Cale's gaze didn't leave hers even when the elevator stopped. A soft *ding* sounded, and the doors slid open.

"Cassidy."

There was no mistaking that deep, grating voice. She'd once thought that a growling bear might sound exactly like Bruce Mercer.

She turned her head, finally glancing away from Cale,

and offered Mercer a faint smile. "Hi, Mercer. It's good to see you, too."

His cheeks were flushed. His hands lifted and pushed against the elevator doors before they could slide closed once more. He glared at Cale. "Lane, I'm gonna want you in my office—so don't even think of leaving the building."

"I wasn't." Cale didn't appear particularly intimidated as he faced off with Mercer. She'd seen plenty of grown men crumble before Mercer. But not Cale.

"Come with me." Mercer grabbed her hand and all but yanked her out of the elevator. Then they were double-timing it back to his office. Rushing past his wide-eyed secretary and hurrying to Mercer's private quarters.

Cale called Cassidy's name.

Mercer didn't slow down.

He threw open the door to his office, pulled her inside, then slammed the door behind her.

Mercer whirled toward her. His clothes were wrinkled, his breath rushing out. Fury marked his features. This was the man who'd been a secret right hand to four presidents. This was—

His arms wrapped around her, and Mercer pulled her close.

Stunned, Cassidy didn't—*couldn't*—move.

"I thought I'd lost you," he gritted out. "Just like I lost your mother…"

His voice—the tremors that shook his body—it was the most emotion that she'd ever seen from the man who was her father.

When Mercer had hauled Cassidy out of the elevator, every muscle in Cale's body had tensed.

Mercer needs to get his hands off her. And the guy had just dragged her into his office and slammed the door shut.

Mercer's assistant, Judith Rogers, was standing up, eyes wide, seemingly frozen by the emotional display from her boss.

Cale stalked toward that closed office door.

Only to find his path blocked by Drew. "You might want to back off for a while," Drew advised him.

He was tired of Drew's warnings And tired of feeling like Drew knew Cassidy better than he did.

"Get out of my way," Cale snarled.

Drew shook his head. "Things aren't always the way they seem."

"Yeah? Well, Mercer doesn't get to intimidate Cassidy—an asset. That's not what we do here."

Cale pushed Drew aside.

The other agent whistled. "It's your funeral."

Cassidy had been afraid. She'd looked at Mercer with *fear.*

Cale didn't want Cassidy afraid of anything or anyone.

"Wait!" Judith squeaked. She usually sounded confident, in charge—not scared. She was scared then. "You can't go in there!"

Sure, he could. The guards were downstairs. He'd passed them all. There was no one to stop him now. His fingers curled around the doorknob, and he shoved the door open—

And found Cassidy in Mercer's arms.

Fury flooded through him. "Get away from her!" His hands fisted. This? *This* was why Mercer had been so desperate to get Cassidy back? Because he was—

Not Cassidy. This wouldn't happen. "I said, get away from her!"

Mercer's head lifted. Cassidy had gasped and spun away from him.

"Cale, no," Cassidy said quickly. "It's not what you—"

"Shut the door," Mercer snapped at the same time. *"Now."*

Cale had shut the door even before Mercer finished speaking. He'd shut that door and crossed the room because he was going *after* Mercer. So what if the man was the director of the EOD? He wasn't getting Cassidy.

Because I want her.

Cassidy pushed in front of Cale. Her hands lifted and flattened against his chest. "It's not what you think. Cale... Bruce Mercer is my father."

And everything in the room got real, real quiet.

Her father? Her father! His gaze swept over her face, then went to Mercer. The director looked like he could chew nails.

Cassidy didn't bear any resemblance to the man. Nothing. No way was she his daughter. Mercer didn't *have* a daughter. The man had no family. Just his job.

"That information doesn't leave this room, Lane. Do you understand me?" Mercer said. Despite his fierce appearance, the man's voice was...shaken.

When Mercer slanted a fast glance at Cassidy, Cale saw a glimmer of fear in Mercer's eyes.

She's his daughter.

Everything made sense then—finally. Why Cassidy had to get so much protection. Why Mercer had been desperate for her to return to the U.S. as soon as the Executioner appeared. Why so many EOD agents had been sent to secure one asset.

The asset is family.

"You were right," Cassidy said quietly. "I'm not an EOD agent. I'm not even an asset."

Mercer had stalked back toward his desk. Cale saw the man run a shaking hand over his face.

He'd *never* witnessed Mercer acting this way. But then,

the man's daughter—*daughter*—had been held by a brutal killer. If that couldn't shake the director, nothing could.

And I used her as bait. I put her in danger.

Hell.

I am so screwed.

Cale squared his shoulders and looked back into Cassidy's beautiful eyes. "I knew you had secrets." He just hadn't realized that those secrets were this personal.

He squeezed her shoulders and got ready to face his punishment.

A faint line appeared between Cassidy's brows. "Wait.… What's happening?"

He moved to stand across from Mercer. The thick carpet swallowed his footsteps. "Am I out? Is it time for me to clean out my desk?" He should have known that the gig wouldn't last long. So much for being a part of a team again. He'd done this, crossed the line and—

"Mercer, *no!*" Cassidy was right by Cale's side. "I'm the one who wanted to go after the Executioner. I'm the one who—"

"Ian Gagnon."

Cale frowned at Mercer's curt response. "What?"

"The Executioner. His real name was Ian Gagnon. I received a report on him right before you two arrived." He exhaled slowly. "And, Cale, I owe you…" It sounded like the man was choking. "Thank you for protecting my daughter. You took a bullet to keep her safe."

"Barely a scratch," Cale muttered.

"Cassidy's strong-willed, just like her mother was." Sadness there, a whisper that slid into Mercer's voice then vanished. "I knew she was trying to track down Gagnon—for years. Ever since Helen…" He shook his head and turned his focus back to Cassidy. "I had my team looking for him, too, but the guy was like a damn ghost. He'd take his victims, use them, kill them and vanish. I was working to bring him to justice, I swear that I was…I just—I didn't want you in his target range. I wanted you safe."

"But I kept hunting him."

Mercer nodded. "You didn't realize that it wasn't just about the money for him. It was the secrets."

Cale felt his gut clench. He knew where this was going. In this business, the right secrets were better than gold. No. They were gold.

"Helen…her father was an Irish diplomat. It started with her—Helen's ransom was for cash and intel. When her father wouldn't give the man what he wanted, Helen died. Anytime the families didn't share their connections—the classified information that they had at their fingertips—then their daughters didn't come home."

And if this Gagnon had realized *who* Cassidy was to Mercer…the man would've been given access to some of the deadliest intel in the world.

Cale shook his head.

"Now you realize just how much was riding on Cassidy's safety," Mercer murmured.

Yeah, he did.

"And you realize—" Mercer's bushy brows lowered "—how grateful the EOD is to you both for finally tracking down the Executioner. You've just taken down one of the most wanted men in the world." He lifted a finger and pointed at Cassidy. "It was dangerous. It was reckless. It was—"

"You're welcome," Cassidy told him as a smile spread over her face.

Mercer blinked at her, looking confused.

Oh, yeah, she does that to people. Even to her own father.

"Helen can rest now," Cassidy said. "And for once,

I won't dream and hear her begging me for help." She glanced at Cale. "I was supposed to be with her that night. We were supposed to leave the pub together, but Helen had met a guy and she wanted to stay and dance and dance...." Cassidy swallowed. "I was tired. I took a cab home. I *left* her."

And the guilt had eaten away at her ever since.

"I never saw Helen again after that. Not alive, anyway."

So she'd made it her mission to get justice for her friend.

"It's over now," Cassidy said with a nod. "I can move on."

Just what did that mean? Cale realized that he wasn't ready for Cassidy to move past him. He wanted her to stay with him. He wanted *her*.

So what if she was Mercer's daughter? He wasn't afraid of the director. No one was going to stand between him and Cassidy.

"You're safe now," Mercer told Cassidy.

But Cale wasn't so sure about that. Would the EOD director's daughter ever be truly safe? Mercer had plenty of dangerous enemies, and if one of them ever found out about Cassidy...

His eyes met Mercer's. *That's why you keep guards on her, isn't it?* It was also the reason no one knew about her.

But now Cale realized the truth, and he was sure that Drew knew—or suspected.

"I made sure that your apartment in town was ready," Mercer told Cassidy. "I'll get an escort to take you over, and we can finish briefing in the morning."

Briefing? Was that honestly the way that the man talked to his daughter?

"I should have waited," Mercer continued. "But I needed to see you with my own eyes. I had to make sure." His lips twisted. "Well, I'm sure now. You're all right. I'm start-ing to realize you're a whole lot stronger than I believed."

Yes, she is.

Cassidy turned for the door. So did Cale. But Mercer stopped him, calling out, "I'm going to need you to stay a few minutes longer, Agent Lane."

Ah, so he wasn't out of the woods just yet.

Cassidy stepped toward Cale. He caught her hand. "Wait for me. We need to…talk."

The leather of Mercer's chair squeaked.

Cassidy nodded; then she slipped soundlessly from the room.

As soon as she was gone, Cale knew that the gloves would be coming off.

"Agent Lane." Now Mercer was back to his growling, fierce self. "Just what the hell do you think you're doing with my daughter?"

Cale kept his hands at his sides. "You're the one who sent me to down Rio. If you didn't want me near her—"

"I wanted you close because you're a damn good agent. I thought you'd do your job and keep her safe."

"The case is over." They should be clear on this. "But my involvement with Cassidy *isn't.*"

Mercer rose. "An involvement isn't going to happen."

He hadn't been asking for permission.

"The EOD is the most dangerous thing in Cassidy's life. Being my daughter puts a target on her that you can't imagine."

He could imagine plenty.

"What the hell do you think would happen if our en-emies found out that Cassidy was both my daughter *and* that she was involved with an EOD agent? They'd use her against us. They would hurt her. They'd—"

"No one hurts Cassidy on my watch." The words were quiet, cold. Lethal.

Mercer stared at him with a measuring gaze. "That better be a promise, Lane."

It was a guarantee.

"Ready?"

Cassidy whirled at Cale's warm voice. He strolled out of Mercer's office looking like he didn't have a care in the world.

Most people looked terrified after having closed-door meetings with her father.

But Cale almost seemed happy as he reached for her hand and led her into the elevator.

When the doors closed, when they had a precious minute of privacy, she had to know. "Just what happened in there?"

"Mercer and I got a few things straight."

Oh, had they?

"The mission is over."

Did that mean another agent would be coming to protect her? Always another agent lurking in the back of her life, skimming the shadows.

"I've got some time coming my way," Cale continued. "And I...I want to spend that time with you."

Hope—real happiness—began to unfurl within her. "You do?"

He nodded and closed in on her. His fingers slid around her, flattening on the walls of the elevator and caging her in.

She rather liked being caged in with him.

"This isn't about a case. It's about us." His eyes searched hers. "I want you, Cassidy Sherridan."

He knew who her father was—he knew her most closely guarded secret. He wasn't running. He wasn't intimidated. He...

Wants me?

"I want you," she whispered back.

He smiled at her. Her breath caught. The man had a killer smile.

She thought he would kiss her. He didn't. He eased back right before the elevator glided to a stop. But his fingers laced with hers as he led her through the lobby.

She'd always been nervous, scared, when she'd been in that building before. But Cassidy didn't feel scared then. She was with Cale.

He made her feel safe.

They brushed by the guards and headed out into the night.

She caught sight of Gunner and Logan. They were outside, probably returning to their own homes. A completed mission. They could all—

The crack of a gunshot broke the night. Even as the sound filled her ears, Cale was pushing Cassidy to the ground and covering her with his body. She hit the pavement with an impact that rattled her bones.

Again? Won't it ever stop?

But, no, it wasn't stopping. Because she heard more shots, blasting away.

She heard voices yelling. Heard Cale swearing softly above her. He'd pulled his weapon, but he wasn't running to chase the shooter. He was staying with her.

Guarding her.

"Get him! Northwest corner!" Cale yelled. "Now!"

Someone had just taken a shot—several shots—at them. No, wait...had the shot been aimed at Cale?

Or me?

"We're getting out of here." Then he was pulling her up, shielding her as he seemed to do too many times. They didn't run for a vehicle, though, not like before.

Instead, they raced back inside the EOD—back into the safety of that building with its bulletproof glass.

Mercer was running toward them in the lobby. "What the hell is happening?"

Cale's fingers brushed over Cassidy's arm. "Someone just took a shot at Cassidy." Cale's voice was grim.

And Cassidy realized that her illusion of safety had just been shattered.

The case might be over, but the threats to her—because of who she was—were always there.

CASSIDY SHERRIDAN WAS a dead woman.

Rage pumped through the shooter's body, a killing fury that had to be unleashed.

Cassidy wasn't in sight any longer. She'd rushed back inside that nondescript building.

I know about that place. The EOD's headquarters.

Secrets had revealed that location. The right leverage, applied to the right people. With that kind of deadly leverage, anything and everything could be revealed.

Cassidy's agent had rushed her inside. He'd moved too quickly, responding even as the bullet had whistled through the air on its way to Cassidy's heart.

The bullet *should* have hit Cassidy's heart.

But Cale had saved her. How had he known about the bullet? *How?*

The shooter hurried away. A getaway vehicle was waiting. A retreat now, but another attack *would* come, soon enough.

The Executioner wasn't gone. He had one last victim to claim.

Cassidy Sherridan wouldn't get to walk away.

Instead, she would get to join her dear friend Helen in the ground.

Chapter Seven

If he'd moved slower, if he'd ignored the kick in his gut that had screamed of danger, then Cassidy would be dead.

Cassidy sat in Mercer's office, looking dazed and lost in Mercer's leather chair.

Did she realize that shot had been meant for her? He'd shoved her to the ground, and the bullet had sunk into the bricks in the wall—bricks that had been right behind Cassidy.

The shooter had aimed for her heart.

Now Mercer was out there, demanding answers, and Cale had no answers to give him.

"Thank you." Cassidy's quiet voice.

His head jerked up.

"You keep saving me." A ghost of a smile curved her pale lips, but her dimple didn't appear. "It's a habit you seem to have."

He stepped toward her, helpless.

"Sometimes, it feels like I've been in danger my whole life. I've never...never gotten to just walk down a street without a guard on me. Never gone to a football game and sat in a crowd. Never done so much...because I'm Bruce Mercer's weakness." Her lips compressed as the smile vanished. "I learned that fact when I was eight, you see. When I was taken."

Every muscle in his body clenched. "Taken?"

Her fingers drummed on the desk. The move gave him pause—Mercer did the same drumming movement, in that exact position, when the man was in deep thought.

"I was with my mother. We were going on a trip to meet Mercer." She licked her lips as her fingers stopped drumming. "We didn't make it."

He was by her side in an instant. The pain in her voice shattered him. "Cassidy…"

"Mercer has a lot of enemies," she whispered. "You don't get to his position by playing nice."

No, you didn't. And Mercer had been in the business of death for decades.

"I don't…I don't think they meant to kill my mother. Maybe just to take her, too, but she fought them, and one of the men had a gun."

Her gaze was so far away.

"It was raining that day. Perhaps that's why a gunshot still reminds me of thunder."

He wanted her in his arms, but Cassidy looked so brittle then.

So breakable.

"I knew she was dead. With that much blood, even a child knew." She swallowed. "They put me in their van, and they rushed away. I don't… I don't know what would have happened to me if Mercer's men hadn't rushed to the scene so quickly. They followed them. I knew they were there for me when I heard the sound of more thunder."

This was the spoiled princess? *Hell, no.*

"An agent pulled me from the van. Took me away, but I looked back. I saw the bodies left behind. In this business, there are always bodies, aren't there?"

He'd left his share of bodies in Rio.

"I didn't ask for this." Now anger pulsed in her words.

"You and Mercer, this is the world you chose, but I didn't." Cassidy pushed to her feet. "I don't want this."

I don't want you.

He stiffened. Cassidy hadn't said those words. She'd told him less than thirty minutes ago that she did want him, but right then the woman was sure putting off get-away-from-me vibes.

He didn't blame her.

The door opened behind him. Cale glanced over his shoulder. Gunner stood there. With his sniper expertise, Gunner had been the first to rush toward that northwest strike zone.

"Tell me you found him," Cale demanded.

Gunner shook his head. "No. The guy had cleared out before I got up there."

"Sydney's ordering a scan on all the security cameras in the area—she's going to pull in traffic cams, too. She might be able to spot him out there."

"Who's Sydney?" Cassidy asked from her position behind Mercer's desk.

"My wife." Gunner's voice was quiet.

Surprise flickered over Cassidy's face.

Before Gunner could say anything else, Mercer pushed into the room. His face was set in determined lines, and he moved with a hard, nervous energy. "They think that they're going to come to my door, take a shot at my—" He broke off, sending a hard glance toward Gunner. "At my asset? No, no, this does not happen." He pointed at Cale. "Get Cassidy to the safe house on Donaghey—"

"But I want to go home," Cassidy interrupted, voice sharp. "You said my apartment was ready."

"And the shooter might already know all about your home." Mercer shook his head. "No, it's not safe. You have to—"

"I'm never safe. Haven't we learned that?"

The bitterness from Cassidy just seemed wrong.

Mercer flinched.

"I won't ever be safe, not totally." She walked from behind the desk. "And I'm so tired of living in the prison that you make for me."

A prison made of agents, always watching her movements.

"You might not like it, but you're going to have to stay under guard." Mercer had locked his jaw. "Until we can find out who we are up against, you have to keep up with your protection."

Cale could see the fury staining Cassidy's cheeks. "Fine. But I'll choose my agent." She turned, looked straight at Cale and said, "I choose him."

Mercer didn't look particularly surprised by that choice. Gunner did.

Mercer began, "I don't know about continuing your protection with Cale. Drew Lancaster is—"

"Not my choice," Cassidy finished. "Cale is the one who just saved my life. Cale is the one that I want."

Her words made his heart beat faster. Harder.

Mercer crossed to his side, paused in front of him so that they stood toe-to-toe. "You guard her with your life. Got me, son?"

He didn't need Mercer to tell him that.

"I've got *her*." And that was all that mattered.

"Go out through the parking garage. I've arranged for transportation there." Mercer stepped back. He looked at Cassidy and paused as if he wanted to say more.

But he didn't.

How long had the wall been there, blocking the man from actually talking to his daughter?

Cassidy headed for the door.

Cale made sure he was with her every step of the way.

"Cassidy!" Mercer's voice.

She looked back at him.

"I'll find the shooter," he promised her.

Cassidy nodded. "But what happens next time?" Her smile was brittle. "Isn't there always a next time?"

Cale was realizing that for Cassidy, the threats might not ever end.

And that made fury boil within him.

As far as safe houses went, Cassidy had stayed in spots a lot worse than the old converted brownstone.

So when Cale led her inside, when he double-checked the security system and secured the facility, she just stood to the side, waiting.

After all, she knew the drill. Once he'd secured the area, then she'd be able to go and find her designated room— and crash.

How many safe houses had there been for her over the years?

After college, she'd thought that she might finally enjoy some freedom.

That dream had died quickly.

"We're clear," Cale said.

They were clear, and they were alone. Why did that make her uncomfortable? She'd longed to be alone with him *before* the bullets had come blasting toward her.

She'd been terrified.

But Cale… Had his heart rate even increased? He'd seemed so controlled and composed to her. Like the threat of death didn't matter.

Probably because it didn't.

"Why did you choose me?"

She realized that she'd been staring at the floor, lost in

thought, but his question made her gaze rise to him. He was studying her, standing less than two feet away.

"You seem comfortable with Lancaster." The words had a hollow feel. "Why not go with him?"

Why, indeed? She shifted nervously. "Look, if you don't want the assignment—"

He eliminated that two feet of distance in less than a second. "Let's get one thing clear. I don't think of you as an assignment."

Oh. That was good. It sounded good, anyway. Her heartbeat had sure picked up plenty at that news as it raced in her chest. "How do you think of me?"

She and Cale were finally away from the other agents and any prying eyes. The rest of the world was locked out. The stillness of the night surrounded them.

Cale's gaze darkened as he stood before her. "I'm starting to think of you as…mine."

The words were rough, possessive. And they were the last things that she'd expected him to say.

Her drumming heartbeat seemed to stop for a moment.

"I don't know how it happened, I just know it did." His hand rose, and his warm fingers curled under her chin. "I see you, and I want."

She licked lips gone dry. He was voicing her own thoughts. "Cale…"

His head bent, and he kissed her. Adrenaline had held her body tight. Adrenaline, fear, anger… But with the press of his mouth to her, all of her feelings seemed to erupt in an instant.

Her hands rose, curled around his shoulders. She pulled him closer as her nails dug into his shirt. The shirt was in the way. She needed him—

Closer.

He wanted her.

She was desperate for him.

And, for however short of a time it might be, she had him. No interruptions. No distractions. Just Cale and her.

His mouth seduced. It caressed, it tempted. His fingers slid down her body, coming to rest right over the curve of her hips, and she could feel the heat of his touch scorching her right through her clothing.

Cassidy wanted all of their clothing gone. She wanted him.

Two lovers. In twenty-seven years, she'd had two lovers. One had been in college, when she'd enjoyed her brief taste of freedom. She'd thought she loved him.

She'd been wrong.

Lover number two had been another EOD agent. She'd thought the strength he offered was what she wanted.

She'd been wrong.

This need... *Cale*... Wanting him had nothing to do with strength. It had everything do with passion. With a consuming desire that grew stronger and stronger in her with his every touch.

And he was touching her. Pushing up her shirt and tossing it away. Then his fingers—those rough, calloused fingers—were sliding over her flesh, and Cassidy arched into his touch.

The killer after her—the fear—faded away.

Only Cale remained.

Only Cale.

He yanked off his own shirt. When she saw his bandage, a gasp broke from her. They had to be careful...they—

He lifted her into his arms, acting like he didn't even feel the wound.

Okay, so maybe they didn't need to be so careful.

Tough guy.

She loved that about him.

They kept kissing. He carried her, moving down the darkened hallway and entering the first bedroom on the right.

It was dark in there, too. But she liked the darkness. You could hide in the dark. Almost pretend that you were someone else.

She wanted to keep hiding and pretend that her reality wasn't a lifetime of guards and secrets.

His fingers were at the snap of her jeans.

But he was hesitating.

Why?

"If you don't want this," Cale growled, his voice rough and wonderful in the dark, "tell me now."

She smiled, but she knew he couldn't see the movement in the darkness. Her hands rose again. Slid over the muscled expanse of his chest. The man's abs... *Wow.* "I want you."

He jerked open that snap. Slid down the zipper. She'd already kicked her shoes away while he was carrying her.

Cool air whispered over skin. No, that wasn't just air. That was his breath. He'd bent, pressing his mouth over the curve of her stomach. And he was kissing her flesh. Caressing her so carefully.

Like she was something fragile to him, delicate.

She didn't want delicacy. She wanted his passion. Every bit of it.

So her hands wrapped around his arms. She arched her hips against him. "Cale!"

His head lifted.

His eyes glittered in the darkness, blazing with need and lust. Then his hands were rising over her. He unhooked her bra and tossed it—heck, she didn't even care where, right then.

She only cared about—

His mouth was on her breast. He licked, kissed, sucked, and her legs rose and locked around his hips. His arousal pressed against her. Long and hard and straining, and she didn't want to wait. It had never been like this, the need a fire in her blood. She couldn't catch her breath. She could only feel him. All along her body. She wanted him inside her. Was desperate to feel the thrust of his body into hers.

"Easy…" His whisper.

Forget easy. She wanted hard and fast and she wanted *pleasure*. Him. *Now*.

He reached around her, sliding his hand into the wallet he'd yanked from his pocket and pulling out—wait, what? Protection? Had to be. The guy was always so prepared.

Maybe too prepared. But the thought was fleeting. Vanishing quickly in the haze of need that surrounded her.

Then he was coming back to her, pulling down her panties. Ripping open that foil packet and, after just a moment, pushing his aroused flesh right against her.

His fingers threaded through hers. His hands pushed hers back against the mattress. His gaze held hers.

And he thrust into her.

One long, hard thrust that sent him deep into her core.

She cried out, lost in the intensity of the moment. Then he withdrew and thrust again, pushing his flesh right over the sensitive button of her desire.

Her legs tightened around his hips. She met him eagerly, thrust for thrust, and the bed rocked beneath them.

Every fear that she'd had vanished. There was no room for fear. There was no room for anything but the passion between them. The fierce movements of his body, the thrust and withdrawal of his flesh, again and again.

Harder.

Deeper.

Making her lose her mind.

Her body tightened. The pleasure was so close, just out of her reach, but every glide of his body, every thrust of his hips, and that pleasure seemed—

Cassidy cried out as the release hit her. Pleasure rocked through her body and she shuddered, caught up in the maelstrom of release as she'd never been before.

Cale's hold on her hardened even more as he gritted out her name. His hips pushed down, he thrust deeper and she knew that he'd found his own release.

Their panting breath filled the air. She didn't move. Didn't want to. Cassidy wanted to go on holding Cale and feeling the pleasure pulse through her body in sweet aftershocks of release.

Killers. Dangers. She wasn't ready to face the threats around her.

So she just wrapped her arms around Cale. She closed her eyes, and she let everything else vanish.

SYDNEY SLOAN—no, now Sydney Sloan-Ortez—knew the minute when her husband entered her office. She just felt him. The air shifted, and every nerve in her body went on high alert. That was generally her body's instinctive response to Gunner.

Sydney looked up, her breath catching. And, sure enough, Gunner stood in the doorway.

Some people were afraid when they saw Gunner. He appeared hard and dangerous, and he'd sure gazed into hell more than his fair share of times.

But when Sydney looked at him, she never felt fear.

Happiness bloomed inside her as she leaped to her feet. Three seconds later, she was in his arms—her favorite spot in the world.

Gunner held her in a grip of steel, his body trembling lightly against hers. "I missed you," he whispered. For

Gunner, those words were the same as a declaration of love. As far as she knew, Gunner didn't miss anyone but her.

He eased back, and his hand rose to gently caress the curve of her stomach.

Her and the twins.

"How are my sweethearts?" His normally hard-as-nails voice had dropped to a croon.

Sydney couldn't help but smile. Gunner was convinced they were having girls. While he'd been on the last mission, she'd found out that the he was right. She was just waiting for the perfect moment to reveal that news to him.

"We're all just fine," she told him, unable to stop her smile. *Now that you're home.* In the past, she would have gone on the mission with him, working easily in the field.

Dodging bullets was almost as natural to her as breathing.

But with babies on board and her doctor emphasizing the risks of a twin pregnancy, she hadn't been about to jeopardize the safety of her children.

And Mercer had also recently offered her a promotion. Director of Information Retrieval. With a substantial pay raise like the one he'd been tossing around, she couldn't refuse. With the new job, she'd still do some occasional fieldwork, but she'd also have a lot more time to spend at home.

With *her* sweethearts.

She pulled Gunner fully into her office and shut the door. She'd missed him so badly, ached for him every night. His eyes were sliding over her now, and she could all but feel the caress on her skin.

To think…she'd almost lost Gunner. Almost let her own past take him away from her.

No one will ever take him away now.

Because she'd do anything necessary to protect him.

Just as he would her. She knew Gunner would lie for her, fight for her, even kill for her if necessary.

A man like Gunner didn't love easily, but when he *did* love, it was consuming.

"I heard that your team took out the Executioner," Sydney said as her gaze drifted quickly over him, making sure there weren't any new injuries on her man. Taking out the international killer sure hadn't been his original mission, but word had leaked quickly through the EOD once the Executioner had been eliminated.

Instead of answering, Gunner brushed his lips against hers, stealing her breath. Giving her his.

She kissed him back, and finally—finally—some of the fear she'd felt since he'd left for the mission to Rio vanished.

Gunner was used to putting his life on the line. She was used to risking her own life. But now...

Everything was different. And they both had to adjust to their new world.

His fingers tunneled lightly through her hair. His right hand was still over her stomach, and when one of the twins kicked, Gunner jerked in a startled reaction.

Then he laughed.

Most folks didn't even think Gunner knew how to laugh.

They were wrong.

His laugh was rusty, rough, but perfect to her ears.

"Tell me what happened," Sydney whispered. She'd heard about the attack outside of the EOD, too. Because of that shooting, the whole building was on lockdown. She had her tech team scanning the traffic videos of a ten-mile radius, hoping to catch sight of the shooter.

So far, they were turning up empty.

So far.

She wasn't about to give up. She'd expand the search parameters and she wouldn't stop looking until she found a clue that the EOD could use.

"He's dead." Gunner's head tilted to the right. "The Executioner is gone."

"Ian Gagnon." He'd been the man given the deadly moniker of the Executioner, and she'd been the one to determine his real identity. The Executioner had once been a young boy, tossed onto the streets of Paris. No family, no one to ever step forward and claim him, the five-year-old had eventually been adopted…and given the name Ian by his new parents.

When he'd turned eighteen, Ian had vanished from his adoptive parents' home. They'd never seen him again.

Now that he was dead, they never would.

"His men—the few that survived—were taken into custody by the authorities in Rio," Gunner continued. "The hostage he'd taken…Genevieve Chevalier… We got her out in time."

They'd gotten Genevieve to safety, and they'd gotten Cassidy Sherridan back to the U.S. Cassidy Sherridan interested Sydney. Cassidy's file was classified, but not by any normal standards. As far as Sydney could tell, only Mercer had clearance to view Cassidy's records.

It would seem that the woman was a very important asset.

"The hit tonight…" She exhaled slowly. "Was it on Cassidy or Cale?" It wouldn't be the first time that an EOD agent had been targeted.

Not the first time.

Not the last.

"The bullet was meant for her." Gunner sounded absolutely certain. He should be. No one knew bullets and sniper attacks quite like her Gunner. "The trajectory, the angle…if Cale hadn't gotten her out of the way, Cassidy Sherridan would be dead."

But Cale had saved her, and, based on the video footage she'd seen, the man had been enraged as he'd turned back to search for the killer.

Not such a cool, calm response for an agent.

"We need to find out who's after her," Gunner said. "That woman has secrets, and I don't want those secrets causing an agent to get killed."

Gunner didn't trust Cassidy. She wanted to help him, but, well, this was the tricky part.

"Her files have a block on them in the system."

Gunner arched a brow. His lips twitched the faintest bit. "Like you can't get past that block."

She could—in her sleep. But blocks were usually put up for a reason. "Maybe there's something we shouldn't know about her." The last thing she wanted to do was draw any additional risk or attention to Gunner or herself.

Her hand slid over her stomach. When she felt the kick, Sydney didn't jerk.

She smiled.

Gunner leaned forward to kiss her once more. But when he pulled away, a furrow appeared between his brows. "Cassidy Sherridan is under EOD protection. How can we keep her safe if we don't know her secrets?"

Secrets could be a very dangerous thing, as they'd both learned.

And no matter how hard you tried, some secrets just couldn't stay buried. "Maybe I should talk to Mercer." He needed to know that she'd be tapping around in his system.

Or, rather, blowing his little security blocks to hell and back.

"Cale took her to the safe house."

There was a darker note in Gunner's voice. She raised her brows. "What is it?"

His lips tightened. "I don't like this setup."

Because he didn't trust Cassidy.

"Cale is a part of our group," Gunner said. "I don't want him in danger because he's falling for a pretty face. I want to know everything about Cassidy that I can."

It wouldn't be the first time that a well-trained agent was misled because emotions got involved in a case. Sydney liked Cale. She didn't want him at risk, either. She didn't want *any* of the EOD agents put in additional jeopardy. Their jobs were dangerous enough without any intimate betrayals.

She knew that from personal experience.

"I'll find out exactly who she is," Sydney promised. And she would. Either with Mercer's help…

Or on her own.

Gunner laced his fingers with hers. "I missed you."

And her heart had been breaking without him.

CASSIDY WAS ASLEEP in his arms. He'd known the exact instant that she'd slipped away, but he hadn't tried to wake her up. He'd held her and enjoyed the feel of her body against his.

He wasn't the type to just hold a woman in bed. That wasn't him. His sexual encounters were usually fast, hot, with no strings attached.

He wasn't looking for strings.

But Cassidy Sherridan came with miles and miles of strings attached.

Cale turned his head on the pillow, moving so that he could see her as the light of dawn spilled into the room.

No makeup, her hair a beautiful tangle, the woman was so gorgeous that she made him ache.

He'd taken her two more times during the night. Wanted more but he'd known she needed to rest. So when she'd fallen asleep, he hadn't woken her.

But he had wanted her.

With her, he was wondering if he'd always want more.

A slow beeping reached him, and Cale frowned. That beeping was coming from their discarded pile of clothes.

Carefully, because he still didn't want to wake her, Cale climbed from the bed and headed for the clothes. He reached down. Found Cassidy's phone. The photo flashing on the screen was of Genevieve Chevalier.

"Cale?"

Cassidy's voice. Sleepy, husky, sexy.

Damn. Those strings were wrapping around him, tighter and tighter, with every second that passed.

The phone had stopped beeping.

He turned toward her. Cassidy pushed up in bed and smiled at him. "You look good in the morning," she murmured as her eyes slid over him.

Not nearly as good as she did.

But then she frowned. "Was that my phone?" She clutched a sheet to her chest. She didn't need to cover up on his account. "Has something happened?" A thread of fear leaked through the words.

Nothing new had happened. At least, nothing that he was aware of. Cale cleared his throat. "Your friend…Genevieve. She was calling."

Her hand reached toward him, grabbing quickly for the phone. "I didn't even get a chance to tell her goodbye!" Her fingers flew over the phone's surface. "We raced away so quickly that I—"

His fingers closed over hers. "Don't tell her where you are." That was the agent talking, not her lover.

Cassidy stilled. Her lashes rose as she gazed up at him. "Why not? Genevieve is my *friend*. She isn't a threat to me."

Until he could learn more about the attack on her, Cale was viewing everyone as a potential threat. "You were targeted just hours ago. Right now, I'm not willing to risk your safety with anyone. Even your *friend*." Actually, he didn't even want her calling Genevieve back right then. What if the call was tracked? What if—

"Stop it." Her voice came out low and cold. The ice— that had been the way Cassidy talked to him before. Back in the beginning. When he'd just thought she was a society queen and she'd thought he was an overprotective agent.

Only they were long past that.

Weren't they? They'd spent a night burning up the sheets. They damn well *should* have been past it.

"Genevieve is my friend—the oldest friend I've got, and I'm calling her back. Something could be wrong. I *have* to check in with her." She put the phone to her ear, and, a few seconds later, the call connected. "Genevieve?" A false brightness rang in Cassidy's voice.

Genevieve might be her friend, or Cassidy might call the other woman that, but it was obvious to Cale that Cassidy wore a mask for the Frenchwoman. She was pretending—and that telling hitch was back in her voice.

Cale wasn't interested in any false fronts. He wanted the real Cassidy in his bed.

"Genevieve, how are you?" Cassidy asked, still with that too-perfect and happy tone.

He leaned toward her and heard a quick smattering of French in response.

Cassidy laughed. "Yes, I know… I was glad to get out of that hell, too. It was a nightmare." Her voice roughened a bit as she said, "I'm so glad that you got out of there.

I was afraid they'd kill you, Gen." True emotion was in those words. The real Cassidy, peeking out.

The real Cassidy was a hell of a lot sexier than the fake debutante.

He wanted to touch Cassidy then, but she pulled away, shifting toward the headboard.

He wanted her back.

"I'm sorry we didn't get to talk more before I left Rio. The—the agents whisked me away."

His eyes narrowed. Had Genevieve heard that little hitch in Cassidy's voice?

"Since I'm an American citizen, the rescue team had orders to bring me back to the U.S." Another laugh, one with a brittle edge. "So, of course, I'm back in—"

Cassidy broke off because Cale had touched her. He had to. The agent in him demanded that he stop her. Cale put his index finger over Cassidy's soft lips.

She looked up at him, her eyes wide in the faint light.

Cale shook his head.

Her breath whispered out against his finger. Then she gave a little nod.

Slowly, his finger slid away from her mouth.

"Where are you, Gen?" Cassidy's voice was huskier now. "Are you going back to France?"

A beat of silence.

"The U.S.?" Cassidy repeated, sounding shocked. "You're in D.C.?"

Cale was already reaching for his phone. If Genevieve was in the city, then the EOD needed to know about that situation. Genevieve had been targeted down in Rio, Cassidy had been targeted…and now someone was after Cassidy once more.

Would the same fate befall Genevieve? If the threat was related to the mess with the Executioner, then, yes. But…

What if Cassidy had been targeted last night because of her link to Mercer?

"Where are you staying?" Now there was fear in Cassidy's voice. "Yes, yes, I know the hotel. Look, don't leave the room, okay?" Cassidy's fears must have mirrored Cale's. "Why? Because—because there are things happening that you don't know about, Genevieve. I just need you to trust me on this. I've got connections in D.C. People who can keep an eye on you. Just…stay inside for now, okay? *Stay there.*"

Cassidy kept talking as Cale turned away. In just a few moments, he had Gunner on the line. He'd heard the name of Genevieve's hotel, and he rattled it off to the agent. "We need a team there, just as a precaution," Cale added, running a hand over the back of his neck. "Until we can figure out what the hell is happening with that attack—"

"Better safe than dead," Gunner finished bluntly.

Yes. Exactly.

"Especially in light of what Syd's finding."

Gunner's words made a thick knot form in Cale's stomach. "Just what is Sydney finding?"

"That there is no cash tied to any accounts that link back to Ian Gagnon. The man's a ghost, one who existed until he was eighteen and then seemingly vanished." A pause. "You don't vanish like that. Not without a whole lot of help."

The kind of help that might go looking for vengeance?

"We need to find out more about Gagnon," Gunner said. Yeah, they sure as hell did. "I don't want to mark this case as closed, not until we know the truth. I mean…why else would someone come after Cassidy? As far as I can tell, the only trouble your girl has ever had is with the Executioner. Otherwise, she's lived a charmed life."

His girl. Cale's gaze moved to Cassidy. She'd ended

her call. Her skin was pale and perfect in the darkened bedroom.

"A woman like her shouldn't be on the radar of killers," Gunner said, voice considering. "She's not part of our world."

Gunner was wrong. So wrong. But Cale couldn't tell him that.

Maybe the attack had been because of Gagnon and not because of Cassidy's own past.

Maybe.

Maybe not.

"I'm going to stay with Cassidy," Cale said. Like anyone could pry him away from her. "Get Sydney to continue searching into Gagnon's past. If the attack on Cassidy is related to him, Sydney will find the link."

When it came to digging into a person's past, there was very little that Sydney couldn't discover with her computer.

His jaw locked. *What if Sydney starts digging into Cassidy's life?*

He'd have to warn Mercer. Because knowing Sydney…

She'd already started to dig.

He ended the call and put his phone down on the nightstand.

Cassidy rose from the bed, pulling the sheet with her. "Do you…do you think Genevieve is in any danger?"

"I think Gunner and Sydney need to know exactly who they are dealing with." *Mercer's daughter.* "Because I don't want them wasting time on a hunt that won't lead them anyplace."

Cassidy flinched. "Are you going to Mercer?"

Hell, yes, he was.

"Because you don't have to do it." She squared her shoulders. "It's my life, and I'm the one giving you permission." Her gaze held his. "Tell your friends who I really am. I'm tired of the lie. I mean, what more can possibly happen to me?"

More than being targeted for death?

Only...death.

And he realized that he wasn't going to tell Sydney and Gunner the truth. Not yet. He wasn't going to tell anyone.

Because he wouldn't let Cassidy be targeted. The instinct to protect her was stronger than anything that he'd ever felt before.

I won't sacrifice her secrets.

But he would find out who was after her.

Chapter Eight

Logan Quinn rode up the elevator in the elegant D.C. hotel. Music played softly in the elevator's interior. A classic piece that he figured belonged to one of the old masters. His wife loved that kind of music.

He wasn't such a fan. Give him some hard and driving rock any day of the week.

The elevator dinged, and the doors slid open. Finally, he was able to escape from that music. The lush carpeting muffled his footsteps as he headed down the corridor. Genevieve Chevalier was in room 619. He'd agreed to take guard duty for Genevieve because he knew that Gunner wanted to stay close to Sydney.

He could relate. Logan sure wished his Julie wasn't so far away. He'd much rather be with her on the quiet beach in Biloxi than in—

Genevieve's door was ajar, and he could see the telltale red of blood on the beige carpet.

Logan pulled his gun and rushed into the room. "Genevieve!"

A chair was overturned. Bedcovers—bloody covers—were scattered on the floor.

He searched the room swiftly, checking the closet, the bathroom, but Genevieve was gone.

He yanked out his phone. "I was too late," he told Gunner as his heartbeat thundered in his ears. Guarding Genevieve had been a precaution more than anything else. A move just in case that last attack on Sydney had been related to Ian Gagnon.

This wasn't about precautions anymore.

Because it sure appeared as if the Executioner was coming back from the grave in order to keep stalking his victims.

Logan spun away from the scene and headed back into the hallway. That faint blood trail might help them. It might lead them to Genevieve. "Get me an analysis unit out here," he said. "As fast as you can." Every moment that passed put his team at a disadvantage on this hunt.

He could hear Gunner barking orders to the men at the EOD headquarters.

"We've got blood at the scene," Logan said grimly.

Blood and no victim.

So much for leaving the nightmare back in Rio. Genevieve had cheated death once. Would she be able to do it again?

I hope so. Hang on, Genevieve. We'll find you.

He just hoped they found her alive.

CASSIDY JUMPED WHEN she heard the loud banging at the front door. She'd just finished dressing, and she hurried out of the bedroom.

Cale was already at the door. Already swinging it open to reveal—

Mercer and Gunner.

Cassidy's breath caught. The men hadn't called them. They'd just shown up at the safe house.

She knew that wasn't a good sign.

Then Mercer's eyes met hers. "It's time to go, Cassidy."

How many times had he said those same words to her? Over and over in her life?

It's time to go, Cassidy.

At her mother's grave, when Cassidy had stood there, feeling so broken and alone. He'd pulled her away, despite her tears and pleas.

She'd wanted to stay, just a little longer.

It's time to go, Cassidy.

At sixteen, she'd been thrilled because she was finally going to attend a party with all of her friends. She'd been dressed, ready to go.

He'd come to her—arrived in one of those big dark cars that he always seemed to use. The kind that had bullet-proof windows. He'd been afraid that someone had found out who she really was.

He'd taken her away.

No party that day.

It's time to go, Cassidy.

More and more instances rolled through her mind.

He always said the same words. Always looked the same. So grim and determined.

When it was her life that was being ripped apart.

Cale took a step toward her.

Mercer lifted a hand and locked it around Cale's shoulder. "No, son, that would be a mistake." Mercer's voice was steely and hard. Most men backed down instantly when Mercer talked that way. She'd sure seen plenty of agents weaken when he used that tone.

But Cale—Cale shrugged away his hold. "I'm not your son." Then he was stalking toward Cassidy. His gaze met hers. "While you were in the shower, I found out…" The faint lines around his mouth deepened. "I'm sorry to tell you, but Genevieve is gone."

Her heart beat so fast that she was afraid it would rip

through her chest. "Gone?" No, a mistake. Genevieve had said that she'd only arrived in town a few hours ago.

She came looking for me.

Because Genevieve wasn't close to her family, either. They were both alone, two women who'd found a kinship with each other. Genevieve might not know about Cassidy's past, but they were friends. They'd been constants in each other's lives for more years than Cassidy could count.

They were *family,* damn it.

"By the time Logan arrived at her hotel, she was gone." This came from Gunner. He'd stepped inside the safe house, making sure to lock the door. He shot a quick glance at Mercer's stony face; then he studied Cassidy once more as he revealed, "There were signs of foul play at the scene."

"What kind of signs?" Even as she asked the question, Cassidy knew that she didn't really want to hear his answer. She didn't want to hear any more at all.

We were both supposed to be safe. The Executioner is dead. The nightmare should be over.

She might not want to hear the gory details, but Cassidy had long ago learned you couldn't hide the dark and ugly parts of life, no matter how hard you tried.

Cale's arm brushed against hers.

He was at her side.

Gunner and Mercer were in front of the door.

"Blood." Mercer's reply was blunt. "Overturned furniture. The surveillance system at the hotel was dismantled, so we don't know who took her—we just know she didn't go willingly."

But she'd been taken, and so soon after talking with Cassidy. Her lips felt numb as she said, "She wanted us to meet."

Mercer took a fast step forward. "You *told* her that you were in D.C.?"

Cassidy shook her head. "No. I said I wasn't at my place, here. She thought I was—that was the reason she came to town." *She came here for me, but I turned my back on her.* Cassidy forced her chin to stay up. "I told her that I was with a friend. We were together. That I would send someone to watch over her until I could get with her."

Too late.

"If Genevieve went to Cassidy's place in order to look for her, then the perp could have seen her there," Gunner said as his eyes narrowed in consideration. "Seen her, targeted her, then followed her back to the hotel and taken her."

Her face went from feeling too hot to icy cold. "Why?" Her gaze was on Mercer. "If this is about us—"

Mercer gave a fast, negative shake of his head. His eyes darted to Gunner, then right back to her. "Right now, we have to assume Genevieve's abduction and the attempt on your life are both related to the Executioner. That case *isn't* over."

Ian was dead. Just how much more *over* could that get? "We have to find Genevieve." The words were so familiar—because she'd been just as desperate to find her friend back in Rio. *This can't be happening again.*

Mercer nodded. "We will find her. I have a team on the job right now. And Sydney's pulling up every video feed in that hotel's area—anything that she can get her hands on. She'll find an image, a car, something that we can use."

Cassidy realized that her hands had clenched into fists. Fear twisted inside her, growing bigger and stronger with every second that passed. She'd thought that she'd saved Genevieve. That she'd done something right for a change.

But now…

"The city isn't secure enough for you," Mercer told her

in his hard, growling, I-know-best voice. "There's a plane waiting for you at the airport."

Wasn't there always?

"Gunner will escort you to the terminal. Lancaster will be waiting to board the flight with you. In a few hours, you'll be—"

Her fists tightened. Her nails dug into her palms. "I'm not running away from this."

Mercer stalked toward her.

Beside Cassidy, Cale stiffened.

"You aren't being given a choice," Mercer said, his voice like arctic ice. "I let you stay here last night while I assessed the situation, but the danger is too great. You're an asset that won't be compromised."

I'm not an asset. I'm your daughter.

But had he *ever* looked at her that way?

Cassidy shook her head, answering her own question.

Mercer's eyes narrowed. "I'm the director of the EOD. I'm—"

"I'm a civilian," Cassidy shot back at him. "So you have no authority over me."

Surprise flashed briefly in his eyes; then it was shielded by grim determination. "You don't want to push on this."

"Yes, I do." *Push for Genevieve's life? Any day, anytime.* "I'm not getting on any plane. I'm staying here, and I'm going to do everything that I can in order to help my friend."

"And what are you going to do?" Mercer demanded. "What do you really think you *can* do? Like you said, you're just a civilian."

What are you going to do? The familiar question echoed through her mind.

"That's the same question you asked me when I told you I was going after the Executioner," Cassidy reminded him.

The silence in the room was heavy and thick.

Voice growing stronger, she said, "I managed to do *something* with him, didn't I?"

From the corner of her eye, she saw that Cale was watching her. He looked...proud?

But then Cale was moving, in front of her, shielding her.

She didn't need to be shielded from Mercer. It was past time for her to stand on her own with him. She immediately stepped to Cale's side.

"I'll stay with Cassidy," Cale said to her father, his voice hard and flat. "I'll make sure she's protected."

"And if you screw up?" Mercer wanted to know. "Because I can see what's in your eyes, Lane." Mercer's tone deepened. "You're making a mistake. Both of you are, and I'm not going to stand by and let Cassidy pay for that mistake with her life."

For an instant, Cassidy could have sworn that she saw grief flickering across Mercer's face. But that was impossible, wasn't it? Mercer didn't feel like other people. The fleeting glimpses that she kept *thinking* were there...they were just her imagination. Wishful thinking from a desperate daughter.

He'd shut himself off from real emotions years ago.

He'd laughed when she'd been a child. Smiled. She was sure of it. Those memories were there, tucked away so deeply in her mind.

She was sure that he had...once.

"You're off the case, Lane." A jut of Mercer's chin dismissed Cale.

"The hell I am," Cale snarled right back at him.

Mercer straightened up, but he still stood an inch or two below Cale. "I just gave you an order, soldier, and you damn well better follow it."

"I'm not leaving Cassidy!" She didn't imagine the emotion in Cale's voice. The anger and determination were plain to see. *He's so different from Mercer.*

"She's not alone." Mercer jerked his thumb over his shoulder, indicating a watchful Gunner. "She'll have EOD agents watching her 24/7. Those agents just won't be you."

But Cale shook his head. "I'm not leaving her."

Cassidy's heart beat even faster. She'd never seen anyone stand off against Mercer with such intensity. Would Mercer give in? Because she knew Cale wasn't going to give up.

Then Mercer smiled. "Cassidy doesn't know about your file, does she? About the violent tendencies that you have…the control issues. The danger that you both covet and create."

She didn't like Mercer's smile. Too cocky. Too knowing. Too Mercer.

Cale quickly glanced at Cassidy. He turned his stormy blue stare back on Mercer. "If I weren't a little violent, I wouldn't get the job done for you, now would I?"

"But the shrink said you could be dangerous, obsessive." Mercer studied him. "Why is it that you're so determined to stay close to Cassidy? Is she becoming an obsession for you?"

What was even happening? "Mercer, *stop!*"

Frowning, he looked over at her.

She just felt tired as she stared back at him. "Stop. This isn't—"

Her phone rang, vibrating in her front pocket. *Genevieve?* Hope flooded through her as she yanked out the phone. *Yes, yes!* That was Genevieve's picture flashing on her screen. She answered immediately. "Gen—"

A scream cut through Cassidy's voice.

Genevieve's scream.

Cassidy stumbled back.

Cale whirled toward her. His hands curled around her arms, steadying her.

"Help me..." Genevieve begged; her sobs filled Cassidy's ears.

"I will," Cassidy whispered. *I promise.* "Where are you, Genevieve? What's happening?"

"They...want you."

Her gaze met Cale's.

Turn on the speaker. He mouthed the words.

Fingers trembling, she pressed to connect the speaker. Then they could all hear Genevieve's cries.

"He says...h-he says that if you don't come, I'm *mort*." *Mort.* Dead.

"Je ne veux pas mourir!"

Tears stung Cassidy's eyes at those pitiful words. *I don't want to die.*

"You won't," Cassidy promised. "You won't! Just tell me where you are. I can bring help to you."

A train's whistle sounded in the background. The sound was long, mournful.

"Je ne sais pas."

Cassidy swallowed the lump in her throat. *I don't know.*

"Track her phone," Mercer whispered to Gunner. "Get Sydney to triangulate that call's location."

"He says that you have to come for me." Genevieve had switched back to English. She did that when she was upset, a tumble of her mother's English and her father's French. "He...he wants you to meet him. H-he said...said to meet him at midnight, at a park just behind—"

Genevieve broke off, screaming, a pain-filled cry. As if she'd been struck or—

No, don't imagine it, don't. Cassidy's breath sawed from her lungs.

"Behind Dunlay Street and M-Manchester," Genevieve finished, tears nearly choking her.

Cassidy heard Gunner softly repeating the instructions to the person on the other end of his phone.

"P-please…be there, Cassidy…"

"I will," Cassidy vowed.

But Genevieve wasn't there to hear her.

The line had gone dead.

THE CLOCK ON Mercer's desk was ticking far too loudly.

Cale paced back and forth in the small confines of that office, tension and adrenaline pulsing through his veins. Cassidy waited down on the level below him, guarded by Gunner and Lancaster, but—

I need to see her.

Instead, he was being called in for a sit-down with Mercer. Like he needed to deal with office politics right then.

The door opened behind him. Ah, so Mercer had finally joined him. *Let the battle begin.*

Cale's shoulders stiffened. "I'm not letting her go to that exchange without me."

Mercer's sigh carried easily to him. The sigh and the soft click of the door shutting behind the director.

Cale glanced over his shoulder at Mercer. The lines on the man's face were even deeper than they'd been before.

Mercer lifted a hand and pointed at Cale. "You're making a mistake."

It wouldn't be the first time.

Or the last.

"You should cover your emotions better." There sure wasn't any emotion in Mercer's voice as he slowly headed around the desk and eased into his chair. The last time they'd been in this office, yes, Cale had been able to read

Mercer pretty well. The emotions had cracked beneath his surface. This time…the man was far too controlled.

He was dealing with Mercer, the EOD director, and definitely not the father who'd been frantic.

Cale realized that he'd done that same compartmentalizing with Cassidy. *The agent and the lover.*

He damn well wouldn't do it again.

Mercer eased behind his desk. The leather chair groaned as he leaned forward. His watchful stare had never left Cale's face. "Others will read those emotions of yours. If you're not careful, your enemies will use them against you."

"I don't know what you're talking about," Cale grumbled, not about to discuss what was going on personally between him and Cassidy. "But—"

"I'm talking about Cassidy. About the way you look at my daughter." Mercer flattened his hands on the desk's surface. "About what others will see unless you start watching yourself a whole lot better."

Cale's back teeth clenched. "What happens between me and your daughter—"

"Cassidy looks a lot like her mother." Mercer's gaze seemed far away. He looked right through Cale, and at his own past. "Same hair, eyes…even that stubborn chin. Marguerite was so beautiful. The first time I saw her…" He swallowed. "I knew I couldn't walk away from her."

Isn't that the way I feel about Cassidy?

Because he knew that he should step down. Another case waited—plenty of other cases—but he couldn't leave Cassidy.

Wouldn't leave her.

"I was undercover, even then. Pretending to be someone I wasn't." Mercer stared down at his hands. "Always pretending. But Marguerite seemed to see through that."

This was a Mercer that Cale didn't know. So he just stood, watching, waiting to see what Mercer would reveal next.

"I loved her, but I loved my job, too. People counted on me. So many lives. So many…" His lips kicked up into a mocking smile. "But I was young. Foolish. I thought I could have it all. The girl. The job. The danger. All of it. Everything I wanted." The smile faded. "We married in secret."

Married…and had Cassidy.

"But I'd made so many enemies. They found my Marguerite. And took her from me." His hands slapped against the desk. "In an instant, they took *everything* from me. I wasn't even there to tell her goodbye."

Cale felt his muscles turn to stone. This story…the ending…it hit far too close to home for him.

When he'd been a teen, his parents had been taken from him. Not by an enemy, but by a drunk driver. Gone in an instant.

He'd never been able to tell them goodbye. He'd never been able to save them.

So he tried to save others.

Cale's breath whispered from his lungs. "You didn't lose everything that day. You still had Cassidy."

Beautiful, bright Cassidy.

Mercer's eyes closed for a moment. "Because of who I am…what I am…Marguerite died. Cassidy had to see that terrible moment. Just a child, and she had to watch her mother die."

And the memory still haunted her. He knew it probably always would.

"What do you think you can give to Cassidy?" Mercer asked him after he opened his eyes.

Cale stared back at him, no ready answer on his lips.

"You're on the same path that I took. Danger. Enemies." Mercer shook his head. "One of your enemies framed you for murder just months ago. You don't have a safe or easy life."

No, he didn't.

"What will you give to her? More danger? Maybe even the same death that I gave to my Marguerite?"

Mercer looked very tired and weaker than Cale had ever seen him before. "I want Cassidy to be safe. To have a normal life. But she won't have that life with you, Agent Lane."

Because he was EOD. Because he'd learned long ago how to deal quick death to the threats in this world.

"Step back from this case," Mercer told him. "Step back from Cassidy before you do more damage to her than even I ever could."

"The last thing I want is to hurt her," Cale conceded. The words were true, but he hadn't thought ahead. Hadn't thought past the moment of being with Cassidy.

He'd just wanted her.

After so long of being in the shadows of life, she'd been a temptation he couldn't resist. He'd reached out to her.

Taken what he needed so badly.

And hadn't considered the future.

"There is *no* future for you two," Mercer said, seeming to read his thoughts. "Cassidy needs to move away from the EOD, away from the guilt of her past."

Because of her friend's death.

"She needs to find someone safe and settle down."

Another man. Anger had his hands fisting.

"You see that, don't you?" Mercer pressed. "You see that you aren't the right one for my daughter."

He wanted to be. He wanted to be her everything.

"Too violent, too dark and with too much death hanging

on you." Mercer's shoulders slumped. "Don't you think I know? You're just like me."

No. He didn't want to be like Mercer.

"We weren't made to love," Mercer continued. "We were made to break and destroy."

Cassidy couldn't be destroyed. "That's not happening," Cale growled.

"You will let her go," Mercer said. "Because you *don't* want her to break."

Their eyes locked.

"I can pull you from this case—we both know I can." Ah, there was the Mercer he knew—the cold confidence. The hard threat.

But Mercer was right. He *was* the EOD. If the guy wanted Cale tossed from the building, he would be. Armed guards would flood upstairs in an instant at his command. They'd toss him into the street.

Then I'd just have to bust my way back inside.

"But I want you working this one," Mercer continued, surprising him. "Cassidy trusts you. And with her friend's life at stake, I don't want Cassidy any more afraid than she has to be."

Cassidy was already plenty afraid.

"So you can keep working with the team."

Cale's eyes were slits. *Thanks—I was going to do that anyway.*

"But when Genevieve is back, when we have this SOB in custody, then it will be time for you to do the right thing and walk away from Cassidy."

The right thing.

For her.

For him?

"Are we clear, Agent?" There was no weakness in Mercer's voice then. It made Cale wonder if there ever had been. Had it just been an act?

Cassidy must have gotten her acting talent somewhere. But unlike Cassidy, Mercer didn't give away any tells when he lied. The man was an expert at deception.

"Oh, I think you're being pretty damn clear," Cale told him. And now it was his turn to be clear. Cale stalked toward the big mahogany desk.

One of Mercer's brows rose.

Cale wrapped his hands around the edge of the desk and leaned toward Mercer. "I'm not you."

Mercer blinked.

"So don't tell me that I am. Don't tell me what will happen to me or to Cassidy." He kept his voice level with an effort. "You're my boss—I get that. But I'm starting to think that coming on board with the EOD was a mistake."

"Are you, now?"

"Being a free agent worked a whole lot better for me. There was a lot less B.S. to deal with." Like a father who should have *been there* for his daughter. He stared at Mercer—glared at him—then said once more, "I'm not you." Then he turned and walked away.

Because, really, what else was there to say?

MERCER DIDN'T MOVE as Cale Lane stalked from the room. The agent did have a lot of rage inside him, but Cale was pretty good at containing that rage.

If he hadn't been so good at that containment, Mercer figured the guy would have taken a swing or two at his jaw.

The door closed behind Cale.

Mercer opened his desk drawer, carefully moved the papers and pulled out the old black-and-white photo that he kept hidden there.

A photo of Marguerite, holding Cassidy when his daughter had been barely a year old.

I deserved those hits.

The past was gone, and no matter how much he wished that he could change things, there was no going back for him.

Things *would* be different for Cassidy. He'd make sure of it. No matter how many strings he had to pull.

And no matter who he had to hurt.

He put the photograph back in place. The edges were rough. From all the years he'd held that precious memory.

Back then, Cassidy's eyes had lit with love when she looked at him.

When had she stopped looking at him that way?

At her mother's grave...

At the grave site, Cassidy's beautiful gaze had held an accusation. She'd known her mother's death was his fault.

They'd both known it.

Because he hadn't been able to give up the job, he'd lost his family.

He shut the drawer and then pressed a button on his phone to contact his assistant. "Get Lancaster up here," he ordered. Lancaster was one agent who never let emotions slow him down.

Mostly because the guy didn't seem to have any emotions.

Not like Cale. His eyes burned when he looked at Cassidy.

A few minutes later, a light rap sounded at Mercer's door. When Drew Lancaster entered, Mercer waved him forward.

"I have a job for you," he said to the agent.

Drew Lancaster nodded.

I can't trust Cale, but I can count on Drew.

In the end, Drew would do whatever was necessary. He always did.

Chapter Nine

"How long have you had the tracking device?" The quiet question came from Dr. Tina Jamison as the EOD doctor approached Cassidy. "I'm sorry but—I, uh, wasn't given full access to your file." No, of course Mercer hadn't given her that access. Cassidy rolled her shoulders.

"The current device was implanted about six months ago." Not that she'd wanted it implanted. But she hadn't exactly been given a choice.

Dr. Jamison, a petite woman with dark hair, peered up at her from behind the frames of her small glasses. "Sydney checked the signal, and it seems to be operating fine."

Ah, Sydney. That would be the delicate-looking blonde over in the corner. The one huddled over a computer screen.

The one with the too-assessing gaze that kept sweeping back to Cassidy.

"It *is* operating perfectly," Sydney said as she rose. And when she stepped away from the computer, Cassidy finally got a good look at the woman—and her very pregnant body.

Didn't expect that.

"No matter where you go, I'll be able to track that signal," Sydney said with a firm nod. "We can find you."

Good to know. Because Cassidy was going to that drop.

Genevieve was counting on her.

The door opened behind Dr. Jamison. Gunner hurried inside. Cassidy tensed. She knew Gunner was working out the details of the meeting with Genevieve's captor and—

And Gunner stopped near Sydney. As she watched, Gunner lightly rubbed his hand over the blonde's neck.

Sydney's features softened.

Wow. I didn't expect that, either.

Gunner, Mr. I Eat Nails for Breakfast, was with delicate Sydney? Before, he'd told Cassidy that he was married to an agent named Sydney. She just hadn't expected to see the two of them like this. To almost feel the connection running between them.

Yes, that was envy that Cassidy felt knifing through her. Envy because Gunner had emotion blazing in his eyes as he looked at Sydney.

Love.

"I'd like to do some blood work on you," Dr. Jamison was saying, pulling Cassidy's attention back to her. "Just some routine—"

"No." Mercer had a rule about that. One that he obviously needed to pass on to the good doctor here. No blood work was ever performed on Cassidy in this facility. Any checks she needed were privately performed in satellite offices that Mercer set up for her.

Tina's eyes widened. "But, I, um—"

"Mercer just wants to make sure the locator is fully functional," Gunner said as he stepped away from Sydney. "Nothing more, Tina. You don't have to run any extra tests."

Cassidy forced a tight smile. "Right. Nothing more."

Tina hesitated, but then she gave a little nod and hurried from the room.

Sydney skirted around Gunner and closed in on Cassidy. Sydney's gaze was assessing as it took her in. "You're not what I expected."

Sydney wasn't what she'd expected, either. If the lady was with Gunner, shouldn't she be a little package of death and danger?

But the woman didn't look dangerous. She was…pretty. Very pretty.

And her hand was lightly rubbing her belly, as if caressing the child inside.

Cassidy pulled in a slow breath. "A party girl, right? That's what you expected?" Another slow breath. Then she let a big smile take over her face. "I'm just a little tired. Give me a bit…" She forced a light laugh. "And I'll be back on my game."

Sydney's head cocked to the side as she studied her. "You're very good at that."

Cassidy kept her smile in place.

"It's almost like another woman just slipped inside of you." Sydney's voice was musing. "I thought you were an asset, but you'd sure make for an interesting agent."

Cassidy didn't so much as flicker an eyelid.

Sydney leaned closer to her. "Why is your file sealed?" A whisper that didn't carry.

Gunner had taken up a position guarding the door.

"What do I need to know about you," Sydney demanded as steel slipped into her soft voice, "in order to make sure that Gunner isn't put at any additional risk while he's on your detail?"

Gunner…who would be a father soon.

Gunner…who looked at Sydney with love.

"Is this about the Executioner?" Sydney wanted to know. "Or is there something more going on here?"

Sydney just wanted to protect her family. What was so wrong with that?

Cale knew Cassidy's secret.

He won't tell them.

Mercer sure wouldn't.

"Gunner is going on the exchange with you tonight. If I need to make sure you have more backup, if I need to change any of the plans, then *tell* me."

Sydney sounded afraid.

I don't want Gunner going with me.

Because it could still be about more than just the nightmare in Rio.

"Why is your file sealed?" Sydney pressed. "Tell me. Or don't." Anger. "I can find out on my own—it will just take a little longer."

But Mercer would have safeguards in place to block access to Cassidy's file. If Sydney did manage to hack her way through the system, Mercer would find out.

Then what would happen to Sydney?

"I'm no one important," Cassidy said. *No hitch, no hitch.* She was working hard to control that tell. "Just a girl in the wrong place."

Sydney's gaze searched hers. "At the wrong time?"

She nodded.

"Bull." Sydney's blunt response.

Cassidy let her smile fade. "You don't want to dig into my past."

"We've all got darkness dodging us." Sydney edged a bit closer. "I just want to make sure your darkness won't hurt Gunner."

Mr. Tall, Dark and Scary. Who was obviously smitten with the blonde. "Gunner seems to be a man who can protect himself."

"He can." There was absolute certainty in her voice. Then Sydney pressed, "What's your secret? Will it hurt Gunner?"

Yes. "I'm not an agent, and I'm not an asset."

Sydney nodded. "You're a personal link."

"Yes."

She'd made the reveal because she wouldn't let her past hurt these people. Going in blind? No, that wasn't what she wanted.

Wasn't it past time that she stopped following Mercer's orders?

"Personal...to Mercer," Sydney said, seeming to understand.

It was Cassidy's turn to nod. Before she could say anything else, the door opened. Cale was there, looking strong and determined and so sexy that he made her ache.

For a few hours, she'd dared to dream of having something more with him.

Then reality had come crashing down on her. The cold press of reality hurt.

"Is Cassidy's tracking signal set?" Cale wanted to know.

Sydney stepped back, moving with surprising speed despite her pregnancy. "Yes. She's good. We can find her anywhere."

"Good." Cale offered his hand to Cassidy. "Come with me."

Anywhere. No, that wasn't what she was supposed to say. She was supposed to keep playing it cool, uninvolved. So what if Cale was the first man who'd actually seemed to want *her* in years?

Not the false image that she presented to the world. But the real person she kept hidden inside.

Her fingers curled around his.

"We leave in forty-five minutes," Gunner reminded them.

Cale nodded, and then he guided her from the room. He hurried her outside through the narrow hallway. She wondered if they were going back upstairs to meet with Mercer, but—

But then Cale opened a door on the right. He led her inside the small office and locked the door behind them.

He seemed to fill that space. His scent wrapped around her, and she remembered—too vividly—what it was like to be locked in his arms. To be holding him tight in the darkness.

"Mercer doesn't want me near you."

Ah, yes, those blunt words were what she'd anticipated. "I told Mercer to screw off." Cale pulled her against him. The heat of his body seemed to sear her. "I'm not ready to give you up."

Not exactly an undying declaration of love. But...

They weren't talking about love, were they? They had need, desire, and it was a whole lot more than she'd felt in a long time.

"We'll get your friend back. After that, I'll take you someplace safe." His head lowered, and his lips feathered over hers. "But then I want you."

She could feel his need pressing against her. Rather hard for a girl to miss a sign like that.

"Mercer was right...I am dangerous. Violent. I've killed."

She wanted his mouth back on hers. Not a teasing soft kiss, but hard and fierce and deep. A kiss that made her feel alive.

The way he seemed to so effortlessly do.

"I'm not a good man for you to want."

He was the only one she wanted.

"But I *can't* give you up. Not yet." Then he was kissing her the way she wanted. With hot passion, stark need. His tongue thrust into her mouth even as his hands curled around her hips, and he lifted her up against his arousal.

She couldn't ever remember being wanted that completely.

Mercer had asked Cale if he was becoming obsessed.

Cassidy wondered if *she* was because Cale seemed to be in her very blood.

Her fingers pressed into the broad width of his shoulders as she clung to him. They didn't have time, didn't have the privacy for what she wanted.

But she still kissed him...letting him taste the passion that she felt for him. So hot.

"Give me time," he rasped against her lips. "Don't vanish with him, not yet."

She didn't want to vanish ever again.

"Too many people have left before I was ready," Cale said. His mouth was inches from hers. "I don't want to lose you, too."

"You won't." Because she was done running. Cale... she wanted to stay with him. Wanted the passion and the life that others had so easily.

With Cale.

It didn't seem wrong to her. Nothing had ever seemed more right.

"I'm going to stay with you tonight. Every second, understand?"

Yes, she did.

"When this is over, it will be just you and me."

That was what she wanted.

"You and me," Cale repeated.

Those were the words she'd hold tight. They would get her through the danger that was coming.

CASSIDY'S TELEPHONE RANG as they reached the designated meeting spot. The peal made her jerk in surprise, but Cale had expected the call.

Sydney would be monitoring Cassidy's phone, trying to track the call's origin and figure out exactly who they were dealing with.

They'd tried to track the first call but had come up empty-handed. The call had been too brief for them to get a good lock on it.

Maybe this time they'd get luckier.

Cale knew that Gunner watched them from the shelter of the darkness on the left, up on the second story of the squat building located there. As a sniper, he always enjoyed a high perch that let him watch his prey.

As for Drew Lancaster, the man that Mercer had insisted accompany them, he was to the right, cloaked by the trees.

Cassidy fumbled as she yanked out her phone. "Genevieve?"

She hit the speaker button so that he could hear.

"H-he said you didn't come alone." Genevieve's quivering voice. "He can see you, Cassidy. Y-you didn't come alone."

"You never said for me to come alone." Cassidy's voice was so quiet that Cale wondered if Genevieve could hear the response. "And he's—he's my boyfriend, Genevieve. He wouldn't let me come alone. He's stayed with me, ever since we met in Rio."

Silence.

"The man...from the ball?" Then Genevieve sucked in a sharp breath. "No! Cassidy!"

The shot rang out then, blasting toward them. Cale shoved Cassidy out of the way, but then he realized that the shot hadn't been aimed at her.

At me.

He tapped his transmitter. "Gunner, tell me that you've

got eyes on the SOB." Crouching, he backed Cassidy up, making sure to shield her even as he drew his weapon.

"From the northeast, using a rifle." A low whistle from Gunner. "Taking aim on him now..."

A crack filled the air. Only this time, the EOD was the one taking the shot.

"Genevieve?" Cassidy's frantic voice. "Genevieve, please, talk to me!"

He glanced over at her. Cassidy still had her phone out. The device was pressed to her ear as she desperately tried to get her friend on the line once more.

Her gaze met his. Cassidy shook her head.

He bit off a curse.

"Heading to the northeast corner now," Lancaster said in his ear. Cale could hear the uneven thud of the other agent's footsteps.

And then...

Another crack split the night.

The bullet sank into concrete inches away from Cale.

Cassidy screamed.

Cale returned fire, having seen the glint off the weapon too late.

Not one shooter, two. The guys had come prepared for the EOD.

Or else they'd come prepared to kill Cassidy.

Just how many men were they facing in that darkness?

It didn't matter. Three EOD agents could handle just about anything.

He shoved Cassidy even farther behind him and took aim again when he saw that glint.

"I've got him," Gunner said into his ear. "But I'm also seeing two more bodies moving on the ground. You need to get her out of there."

"Northeast corner is empty, but there's blood on the

ground. Gunner got a hit," Lancaster told them in the next instant. "There are motorcycle tracks back here. Fresh, from the look of them—"

He broke off, and the sound of gunfire had Cale's eardrums aching.

A trap.

The hit from the northeast corner had been designed to draw out Cale's team. And, sure enough, Drew had gone right back there—lured by the bait.

"Lancaster!" Now Cale was the one trying to frantically get a response.

"H-hit," Lancaster responded weakly. "Get...out..."

The EOD didn't leave a team member behind. That wasn't how they worked.

But he wasn't going to risk Cassidy, either. These bastards wanted her, but they'd have to go through him in order to get her.

"Give me cover, Gunner, and get backup out here—"

"Sydney's already got it on the way."

He kept a tight grip on Cassidy's wrist. "Move with me. Every step."

She nodded.

Then they were off, rushing back through the dark woods, heading for the safety of the SUV that waited near the street and—

"Cassidy!"

Cassidy froze.

"No! Keep going!" Cale ordered.

She tried to pull away from him. "That's Genevieve!"

It was another trap. One designed to bring her into the darkness, the same way that Lancaster had been lured in. Only...

"There's no exchange planned. He's not going to let her go. He'll take you both." She had to see that.

Cassidy stared back at him. "But we knew that was the plan all along, didn't we? That's why you're here. Why I'm here. Why I've got the tracker."

His jaw ached.

"So let's do this." She yanked her hand away from him. "Just follow me. She's *here*."

And Cassidy could be tracked anywhere.

Then a hail of bullets broke the night.

No! Cassidy could be tracked, but if a bullet took her out… More gunfire told him that this wasn't about capturing Cassidy. Not about using her.

It was about killing her.

And Cassidy was running away from him. Running toward Genevieve's fading scream.

"No!"

He had to go with her.

Cale lunged after Cassidy.

And that was the moment when the world exploded around him. They'd planned carefully, wearing bulletproof vests, putting Gunner up for surveillance… Even Mercer was staked out just a block away.

But they hadn't counted on the bomb.

It lit the whole night.

The force from the blast lifted Cale up and tossed him back, away from Cassidy. He yelled her name, desperate, as he slammed back down into the earth.

But Cassidy didn't answer him.

And as the flames flickered and spread, he shouted for her, again and again.

FOUR DEAD BODIES were recovered at the scene. Four men in black, men who'd been taken out by Cale and Gunner's bullets.

Four bodies, but no sign of Genevieve or of Cassidy.

"You were supposed to protect her!" Mercer snarled, spittle flying from his mouth.

They were still at the scene. The heavy scents of ash and blood filled the air.

He'd expected Mercer's fury. The same fury—and fear—were coiling dangerously within him. *Where is Cassidy?*

"Get Sydney to activate her tracking device." That was the plan, right? He glared at Mercer. "This was your idea. You were the one who wanted—"

To use your own daughter.

But I was the fool who agreed to the plan. Because Cassidy had been so desperate to get her friend back.

Mercer glared at him. An ambulance's swirling lights flashed. "You said you'd keep her with you every single minute."

"Get the track going!"

He spun away from Mercer before he gave in to the urge to drive his fist right into the man's face. When he turned, Cale saw Lancaster being loaded into the back of an ambulance.

"The track's on." Sydney's quiet voice. *Sydney's here?* He looked to the left and saw Gunner holding her within the protective circle of his arms.

"Cassidy is three miles over, heading east on Brookley." *Hell, yes.*

"We've got a link on her and—" Sydney broke off, frowning at the small monitor gripped in her hand.

"Sydney?"

She looked up at him, frowning. "We lost the signal."

"Then get it back!"

She started typing quickly on the keypad. She tapped her transmitter, talking with her team back at the EOD office.

A heavy cold began to spread through his gut. "Sydney?"

She shook her head. "Her tracking device went off-line."

Fear was driving his rage, breaking his control. Cassidy never should have been there. He'd told her and Mercer the plan was crap. "Why? Why isn't it working?"

Sydney licked her lips. Her gaze darted over his shoulder. To Mercer? "I don't know."

CASSIDY SCREAMED WHEN the knife plunged into the curve of her shoulder. A man's rough hands held her down, forcing her against the side of the van.

The van. The big, black van that had been waiting for her after the fire had erupted, separating her from Cale.

Cale!

"Let's see them find you now," the man muttered.

They'd taken out her tracking device. They'd known *exactly* where the device was located. *How?*

"We know your secrets, Cassidy Sherridan," the man told her as he ran the bloody tip of his blade over her cheek. "And soon we'll know your father's secrets, too."

This wasn't about the Executioner. *We were wrong.* Genevieve had been taken...Cassidy had been taken—because of Mercer. Not because of the killer in Rio.

The van bumped and jostled, and Cassidy remembered another night. Another time.

It had been a van back then, too. A big white van. A delivery van. It had been broken down in the middle of the road. Her mother had stopped to see if she could help the driver.

Then the men with guns had jumped from that van.

Her mother had screamed for Cassidy to stay in the car.

The car hadn't been any protection.

"What will the big man do in order to get you back?"

Her mother had fought. She'd been so desperate to protect Cassidy.

She'd fought and she'd died.

"Where's Genevieve?" Because she'd heard her friend's screams. They had pulled her away from Cale. Genevieve had *been* there in that park.

"She didn't survive the little rendezvous with you." Mocking laughter from him. From the man that she still couldn't see. "But don't worry, your Genny did her job just fine. She brought us you."

Genevieve was dead? It felt as if he'd just shoved that bloody knife right in her chest.

No, Genevieve should have been saved. It had been a rescue mission.

The van bumped again. Her blood soaked her shirt. Her shoulder throbbed. Burned.

"You'll tell us everything," the man ordered, his voice low and sinister. "Everything you know about your father...*and* your lover. We know Cale Lane is EOD. You'll tell us about him, about them both."

And she'd still die.

Her mother had fought.

I am my mother's daughter.

They should have checked her for weapons. They'd made the same mistake that Cale had made before. Story of her life—always being underestimated.

Their foolish mistake. She hadn't walked into that park unarmed.

She was sitting with her legs curled toward her body. This time she wasn't packing a knife in her ankle holster. Her boots hid a small gun that was secured to her ankle. Her right hand slid down, and her fingers locked around the weapon. "Get away from me."

He laughed.

"Let me go!"

"No. I'm going to make you scream."

The way her mother had screamed? *Screamed for me to hide. Screamed and said, "Close your eyes, ma petite. Close your eyes!"*

Only Cassidy hadn't closed her eyes.

She didn't close them now, either. She yanked up that gun, and she fired at him.

The bullet tore right through him and flew toward the front of the vehicle.

Cassidy's captor stumbled back, roaring in pain and shock.

And another cry, pain-filled, just as shocked, came from the front of the vehicle. Then the van swerved, twisted—

Cassidy leaped to her feet. She shoved open the back door of the van. Wind whipped against her body. This was her chance. She was taking it.

The black pavement blurred beneath her eyes. It would hurt. But pain was better than dying.

She sucked in a sharp breath.

"No! Stop—"

Cassidy jumped onto the pavement. She hit hard, rolled and felt the flesh tear from her hands and arms.

The van slammed on the brakes, and the scent of burning rubber filled her nose. Cassidy knew that she had to get up, she had to run, so she staggered to her feet. She stepped forward—and fell again. Her ankle throbbed painfully.

Then she heard the sirens. The sweet, beautiful sirens that were getting closer, closer, and she lifted her head and just saw the flash of red lights coming toward her.

She tried to crawl toward those lights.

The van's tires squealed as the vehicle rushed away.

Cassidy kept crawling toward those lights.

CALE SHOVED DOWN the brake the instant that the patrol car's headlights fell on Cassidy. He'd taken that damn vehicle, rushed over to Brookley, burning rubber, and he'd desperately searched the surrounding streets.

His palms were sweating, his heart racing.

And Cassidy—his Cassidy—was crawling in the middle of the road.

He threw open the door and rushed toward her. "Cassidy!"

He'd raced to another scene, on another street, so many years before. He'd found the bodies of his parents.

Seen his little sister…

She'd been alive.

So was Cassidy.

HE LIFTED HER into his arms. She was bleeding, trembling. He wanted to crush her to him, but he forced his hold to stay gentle. She needed care from him right then. Not raw desperation. "It's all right, sweetheart. I've got you."

"They…knew…"

He carried her back to the patrol car. His breath hissed from between his teeth when he saw the blood on her shirt. Too much blood. "Cassidy…"

"He cut…tracker…"

He grabbed for his phone. "I've got her." What street was he on? "Debouy and Hutchins. She needs an ambulance!" And if that ambulance didn't get there in the next few moments, he'd just rush her to the hospital himself.

Cassidy…bleeding out in his arms. *Nightmare.*

That wouldn't happen. He'd said that he would protect her.

"C-Cale?"

His body had curled over hers. He'd put his hand over

her main wound, applying pressure to stop the blood flow as best he could.

When he'd been back at that park behind Dunlay, dark fear had controlled his thoughts.

Cassidy had left him. He hadn't gotten to tell her good-bye. Just like with his parents.

His lips brushed her cheek. "Don't leave me."

Her hand rose. Her fingers—her skin had been scraped from her palms. What the hell had happened to her? But her fingers lightly touched his cheek. "I'm...not." She even tried to smile then. Smiling? After what she'd been through?

His heart stopped for a moment.

Then beat even faster, harder, than it ever had before.

"It takes more than...this," Cassidy whispered, "to stop me."

And he knew that he was staring at one of the strongest women he'd ever met, and he'd sure come across more than his share of fierce protectors during his time in the military—and as a civilian.

Cassidy wasn't weak. She was—

Everything.

He held her even tighter. "Tell me who did this to you." He could hear the scream of the ambulance's siren, coming closer and closer. "Tell me, sweetheart. I'll find them." Hunt them. Stop them.

Kill them.

No one hurts her and walks away.

Yeah, that violent side of his, that predatory side that others whispered about? That Mercer had flat out taunted him with? It was out.

He'd been trained to hunt and kill his enemies. The one who'd done this to her would pay.

Cale would make absolutely certain of that.

"I shot him," she confessed in a whisper.

His eyes widened.

Good.

"I had…a gun…at my ankle. Got it before I—I left… the EOD."

The ambulance rushed around the corner and came to a screeching halt. Two other vehicles were right behind it—a black SUV and a long, gray sedan.

The ambulance attendants ran toward them. Gunner and Mercer jumped out of the SUV.

"Never saw his face…"

"Cassidy!" Mercer was there, shoving *back* the ambulance attendants.

Cale growled at him. "Let them through! She's hurt!" He had her blood on his hands.

"S-someone else was driving…the v-van…d-dark van…" Cassidy told him, voice roughening. "Two people…two…"

After the way things had gone down at the park, he'd realized they were dealing with a group, not just one attacker.

A sob burst from Cassidy. Mercer had moved back, finally, and he stood watching them, with his hands clenched into fists. "G-Genevieve…" Her name seemed torn from Cassidy. "She's dead."

Cale's breath was cold in his lungs. He'd been afraid that she was.

The captors had gotten Cassidy, and once they had her—well, Genevieve was no longer an asset. She was another body to carry around—a liability.

Deadweight.

He helped the attendants load Cassidy onto the stretcher. She held tightly to his hand, her grip fierce and desperate.

His hold on her was even stronger.

Mercer stood to the side, watching, with shoulders slumped.

"She was my f-friend," Cassidy whispered as tears tracked down her cheeks. "The only one I had, for so long."

Her tears were ripping him apart. "You're not alone, Cassidy. I won't ever let you be alone." No matter what he had to do. No matter what he had to sacrifice.

His life—everything—had changed for him.

"How bad is it?" Mercer asked quietly.

Bad enough. There was too much blood. Cassidy was too pale under the ambulance's lights.

"Blood pressure's too low," one of the attendants said. "We need to get her to the E.R."

"I'm going," Cale said instantly. And he was. When that stretcher was loaded into the ambulance, he was right there.

At her side.

Where he knew he was supposed to be.

He brushed the hair back from her cheek, wiped away her tears.

When Cale looked up, he saw Mercer standing just past the open doors of the ambulance. "Stay with her, Agent Lane," Mercer ordered, his voice gruff.

No emotion there. Emotion *should* have been there. The guy was her father. He should be trying to get in that ambulance, too.

But Mercer was stepping back.

"I'll want to talk to her when she's clear," Mercer added with a firm nod.

The guy was acting as if Cassidy was any other asset. *She's not.*

Cale glared at him. This guy held most of the power reins in D.C., but folks didn't realize it. Cale realized it. He wasn't intimidated.

He was furious.

"Get your damn priorities in order," he snarled at him.

Then the doors closed.

He couldn't see Mercer anymore. Good. He didn't want to deal with Mercer then.

Only Cassidy mattered.

"C-Cale?" Cassidy was shaking.

No, seizing.

When he heard the EMTs say that her blood pressure was dropping too much, Cale felt his own heart start to sputter with fear.

He held her even tighter. As the medics worked on her, as they tried to stabilize Cassidy, he held her tight.

Because she wasn't just an asset to him.

MERCER WATCHED THE ambulance rush from the scene. He swallowed the lump that wanted to choke him. When he'd first seen Cassidy, cradled in Cale's arms, with all that blood…

I thought I'd lost her, too.

"Mercer?" Gunner's quiet voice. "I saw a video camera on that last red light that we passed. I've already called Sydney—she's gonna pull up the feed."

And Sydney would be able to show them all just what had gone down on that dark road. Just how his daughter had wound up bloody and broken.

He tried to control the rage growing in him. With his job, he wasn't supposed to let emotion rule him.

He wasn't supposed to—

Marguerite had looked as broken as Cassidy. With blood on her body. So pale. Just left in the street.

Like his Cassidy.

His fingers were shaking. Mercer balled them into fists.

"Sir?"

Had he spoken? He must have, because Gunner was frowning at him.

"We find them. We take them out." His words were brittle. "I want every tech we've got going over that video. We'll put an all-points bulletin up for the vehicle, and we will have that van." He wanted that van found within the hour. The video would show them the make and model of the vehicle Cassidy had described. "Cassidy shot one of the assailants, so he'll need medical help. Get men at the hospitals. Anyone comes in with a gunshot wound, I want to know about it."

He paused, sucking in a sharp breath as he realized that his words had fired out too hard and fast.

Not controlled.

Not any longer.

Cassidy's blood stained the street.

Gunner stepped closer to him. "Mercer..."

"Cale can't be trusted to keep her safe." Flat. He believed those words with every fiber of his being. Because he'd seen the way the man looked at Cassidy when she was loaded onto that stretcher. That look wasn't just about attraction.

It was much more.

Once, Mercer had looked at Marguerite that way.

When emotions got involved, the cases became even more dangerous.

He didn't let Gunner and Sydney work in the field together any longer—he couldn't. It was too much of a risk. But Sydney had been promoted to oversee their tech ops, and Gunner...well, Gunner had already shown signs of wanting to pull away from the EOD.

Few agents stayed with the EOD for life.

"I think you're wrong." Gunner's voice was quiet. Intense. The way the guy always seemed to be.

Mercer glared at him.

"I think Cale is actually your best bet for keeping her safe right now."

Bull. He was a liability. Despite any of Mercer's original plans, the situation had changed. "Why would you—"

"Because I've got eyes, too, Mercer. If someone tried to hurt Syd, what do you think I'd do?"

He knew exactly what Gunner Ortez would do. *Kill.* Because Sydney and the twins *were* Gunner's life.

But Cale had only just met Cassidy. His feelings for her couldn't be trusted. They'd make him weak. They'd—

"He won't leave her. You can kick him out of the EOD, you can try to force him from her side, but the man is one of the most dangerous I've ever met. We'll waste more time trying to stop him from being with her than doing anything else."

Gunner was trying to be reasonable.

Mercer was tired of reason.

"He'll destroy her." Said with certainty. Because Cale was too much like—

Me. And I destroyed my Marguerite.

"Sometimes people can surprise you."

Mercer marched away from him. Techs had arrived on scene. They were studying the skid marks left on the road. They'd already flagged an area of blood on the cement.

Cassidy's blood. He hated the sight of her blood.

"People don't surprise me anymore," Mercer muttered. He knew all about the darkness inside them. There were no surprises. In the beginning, he'd actually thought that Cale might—

He stopped the thought. No, Cale wasn't good for Cassidy. Cale was too much of a threat. Steps would be taken to separate them.

Cassidy would be safe.

Cale would be sent on another mission.

Life would go on.

It always did.

Except for my Marguerite...

Her life had ended far too soon.

"Find them," Mercer ordered the men and women who stared at him with wary eyes. *Kill them.* Because if her attackers knew Cassidy's true identity, then he couldn't allow those men to live.

He didn't need Cale to tell him about priorities. His main priority was the same one that it had been since the day he buried Marguerite.

Keep my daughter alive.

Nothing else mattered.

No one else mattered.

Chapter Ten

The lights in the hospital were too bright and hard, glaring down on her as Cassidy lay on the operating table. She wasn't shaking anymore. That was good, right? She was sure trying to take it as a good sign. The violent tremors had rocked her for so long, and she'd been terribly afraid.

I don't want to die.

There were too many things that she wanted to do in this world. Death wasn't an option.

Please, don't be an option.

An IV fed into her wrist, she wasn't sure why, and there was a circle of doctors around her.

"Cale?" She needed him to be there with her. Her head turned a little to the right.

And she saw that he was. Stepping quickly to her side. Sliding his hand over her cheek.

The heartbeat that had begun to race slowed down. The beeping machines quieted a bit.

"They're almost finished stitching you back up," he told her.

It seemed like every time she turned around, she was getting stitched up—or he was. Couldn't they manage to go a few hours without injury?

But Cassidy didn't want to think about stitches or wounds then. She could feel the slight pressure on her, but she didn't try to look over at the doctors.

She kept her eyes on Cale.

Genevieve is dead. A hollow ache filled her chest. She'd lost someone else that she cared about. Sometimes she felt like she was cursed. Always meant to be on her own.

Genevieve had deserved better than to die because she knew Cassidy.

I should have gone to her. As soon as Genevieve had called her, Cassidy should have run to her.

But she hadn't.

She'd been too busy keeping her secrets. How many lives would her secrets cost?

"Th-the other agent," Cassidy whispered as worry pulsed through her. "Drew Lancaster. How is he?" *Be alive, be—*

"Lancaster's fine. It takes more than a bullet to stop him."

But one slice of a knife had almost taken her out.

"Cass." He breathed her name like a caress. "What happened to your hands? Your knees?"

She tried to smile for him. "I jumped out of the van."

His eyes widened.

The pressure on her wound finally stopped. Cassidy pulled in a deep breath. "Get me out of here," she whispered to Cale. "Please, just *get me away from here.*" Away from the death. Away from those bright white walls. Away from the nightmares that just wouldn't stop.

Cale stared into her eyes, then, after a brief moment, he nodded.

Thank you.

"I NEED HELP!" His voice was high and shrill. Desperate. Angry. Pain-filled.

Probably because his blood was pouring all over the back of the van.

"Take me to a hospital!"

That wasn't going to happen—he should know better than to even ask for such a foolish thing. The EOD would already have eyes at all of the hospitals, waiting for a gunshot victim to be brought in.

Cassidy had been surprising. She'd actually used her weapon, been ready to kill in order to survive.

I didn't think she had it in her.

But perhaps Cassidy was like her father, after all. Mercer had never hesitated on a kill.

No matter how many lives he destroyed.

"Help me!" He was clutching his stomach, moaning. He could survive the wound provided that he got help soon enough. The blood flow could be staunched. He'd get stitched up.

But he'd be weak.

There wasn't time for weakness. Already agents were probably tracking the vehicle. Those stupid cameras were everywhere in the U.S. Big Brother—Mercer—always watching.

But the screaming man had to be dealt with. It was so hard to find good help these days. So hard...all of the best men in their team had died in Rio, courtesy of Cassidy and the EOD.

"Please!" he gasped out.

Fine. "I will help you."

He smiled. Finally stopped that pathetic begging. Good. His calm would make things easier.

He didn't see the gun—not until it was too late. By

then, there was no time for any more pleas. No time to try to lunge away.

The bullet hit him in the heart. A direct shot. Not sloppy aim. Cassidy had been sloppy.

He fell back, his head slamming into the floor of the van.

Injured, he'd been a liability. He would have kept demanding help, and if he'd gone to the hospital, then Mercer's men would've had him.

The injured man would have turned on his boss—it would only have been a matter of time. The loyal men had died in Rio. The others…they weren't to be trusted. Used, but not trusted.

The smell of his blood deepened in the air. Cassidy had bled in that van, too. Bled, pleaded.

Escaped. Damn it.

The hunt wasn't over.

Not yet.

An eye for an eye.

The scales were far from being balanced.

The van was left just where it sat, its doors hanging open. Mercer could find the dead man inside. A dead man would tell him nothing.

Cassidy would be in the hospital. Which one?

Doesn't matter. I'll keep looking until I find you.

Cassidy might have thought that she'd gotten away clean, that she could just disappear with her agent lover, but she was wrong.

An eye for an eye.

Cassidy was going to find out that there was no escaping from death.

SHE'D WANTED OUT of the hospital, but that wasn't happening. Cale had agreed to take Cassidy away, but he had to make sure she was recovered enough first for the travel that he had in mind.

The staff gave her a private room. Mercer sent guards for her, and Cale didn't leave her for even a moment.

She slept. He stood watch.

Against those white sheets, she looked too pale and fragile. So very breakable.

He wasn't going to let her break.

The door squeaked open behind him. He turned instantly, moving for the weapon that was still holstered beneath his shoulder. An instinctive response.

But it was Dr. Tina Jamison who stood in the doorway. He frowned at her.

Tina didn't usually leave the EOD headquarters for a case. He'd actually only seen her in the field twice, both times to help wounded agents. She'd been scared each time, her hands trembling, but she'd gotten the job done.

"Mercer. He wanted me to come in and make sure that Cassidy was all right." She pushed the door closed behind her. "He also wanted me to check on you."

He was barely aware of his own wounds, some scratches and contusions from the blast. The docs at the hospital had patched him up, too, despite his protests.

Tina headed toward the monitors on the right side of the bed.

"The docs gave her a sedative to help her sleep."

Tina paused, then glanced back at him. "Is that what they told you?"

He didn't like her tone, not a bit. Suspicious now, he kept a wary eye on her.

Tina reached for the clipboard. "It looks like she'll be just fine." She put the clipboard down and turned to face him. "Now let me check on you."

Cale grabbed the hand that lifted toward him. "What's going on, Tina?"

She glanced down at his hand. He felt the tremble that shook her. No, Tina didn't like leaving the safety of her labs at the EOD. But she'd come there tonight, on Mercer's order?

Is that what they told you? Her words rang in his head again.

"What's going on?" He wanted to know. He and Tina hadn't exactly gotten close during his time at the EOD. Tina and Sydney were tight, though, best friends from what he could tell.

"I'm following orders," Tina said. "We all have to follow orders, don't we?"

He was getting tired of the orders. Before he'd joined the EOD, he'd been a free agent working to help those who needed him. A mercenary? Maybe he hadn't liked that title. Maybe he'd wanted to see what it would be like to be part of a team.

And being a Shadow Agent did have its moments.

But it could also—

"If Cassidy was awake, she'd fight."

He almost missed Tina's whispered words.

But as they sank in, a cold fury spread within him. "What's happening?" As if he didn't already suspect— *Mercer.* The director was happening. His schemes and plans.

"A transfer team is waiting outside. Since her location in D.C. has been compromised—" serious understatement "—Mercer wants her taken out of the city. When she wakes up, Cassidy will be far away."

He shook his head in denial. "Mercer didn't tell me about any transfer. He didn't—"

"That's because you're not going with her." Tina didn't look him in the eye as she revealed this information.

The hell he wasn't.

Tina stared at his neck. "He says the threat to this asset is too strong. That she has to be relocated before her position can be compromised again."

This wasn't happening. "You're just going to take her while she's unconscious? While she can't say or do anything to stop you?"

"It's not me." Her gaze flew back up to hold his. "You have to understand, Mercer is—"

"Screw Mercer!"

She flinched.

No, he couldn't take his fury out on Tina. He brushed by her and went back to the bed. "Get the IV out of her."

Tina didn't move.

"Get it out, Tina!" Because that IV was pumping the drugs into her body. Not to stabilize her, as he'd been told, but to keep her unconscious so that Mercer could whisk her away again.

Cassidy's weak voice whispered through his mind. *Get me out of here.* Had she made that plea because she knew what Mercer would do? Had he done that to her before?

Probably.

But he wasn't doing it again.

Cale heard the light shuffle of her footsteps as Tina inched closer to him. "If you go against Mercer, you know what will happen."

He could kiss his career in the EOD goodbye. *Fine. Whatever.* "It should be her choice." That was exactly what it *would* be. She would be awake. Aware. Cassidy would be able to choose—the path Mercer wanted for her, or...

Me.

Because he could protect her. If she needed to get away

from D.C., then he could make that happen. He already knew exactly where he wanted to take her.

Home. Whiskey Ridge, Texas. The only home he'd ever known.

"I—I—" Tina's halting steps stopped. "He said she was in danger. That we had to move her."

And Tina was following orders, trying to protect a civilian.

"Get the IV out of her." Or he would. He just didn't want to hurt Cassidy. But one way or another, that IV was coming out.

He looked over his shoulder and leveled his stare on Tina. Waited. "It should be her choice. You know it, and I know it."

Tina gave a small nod.

Then she reached for the IV.

GUNNER APPROACHED THE VAN slowly, his weapon up, two other EOD agents at his back. They'd kept regular law enforcement personnel in the background as much as possible—not like it had been easy to cover up the explosion in the park.

The van's back doors hung open, its cavernous interior dark.

As the men closed in, one agent swept a light inside.

The light fell on a dead body.

Gunner's eyes narrowed. Two shots. One had hit the man in the stomach. One had blasted right into his heart. From the look of the wounds, both had been administered at a very close range.

Cassidy had told Cale that she shot her attacker—that she hit him *once*.

Had she been mistaken, or had another scene played out here?

His gaze searched the van. No driver. But someone *had* been behind the wheel while Cassidy had been held captive in the back.

His stare returned to the body.

Cassidy shot him in the stomach. That would make sense. The first bullet, ripping through him, gave Cassidy the precious moments that she'd needed to escape.

But that wound hadn't killed him.

The wound to the heart had ended the man's life.

His partner shot him in the heart.

It was the partner that they had to find.

He turned away from the van and began to slowly scan the street. He was good at tracking, almost as good as his grandfather had been. He'd been trained on the reservation as a child, and when it came to hunting, he did the job well. Maybe too well.

Gunner crept to the edge of the road. Let his light sweep over the grass.

There. Bent grass, broken by feet running too quickly.

He followed those telltale marks. The bent grass, the snapped twigs.

The driver had come this way for a reason. He'd abandoned the van in that spot for a reason.

A few more feet, and he found that reason.

Tire tracks. A second vehicle had been stashed there.

The killer was on the move again, and he could very well be closing in on Cassidy.

CASSIDY'S EYES SLOWLY opened, the green color muted, her gaze confused. "C-Cale?"

He didn't like the slur in her speech. He'd been right there, right beside her, and she'd been drugged.

He couldn't believe Mercer had been dumb enough

to think that Cale would let her walk away. Or just be *taken* away.

"What's happening?" Cassidy asked as she tried to sit up.

He put his arm around her, helping to steady her. He'd already dressed her—well, done his best, anyway—in jeans and a T-shirt that he'd gotten Tina to sneak up from the gift shop. "Mercer wants to take you out of D.C." There was no time to sugarcoat. He figured they had all of about five minutes to get a plan in motion.

Mercer moved fast.

So did Cale.

"Out of..." Cassidy put a hand to her head.

"You have a choice to make." He kept his voice steady. Kept his hand on her arm because she was weaving a bit on the bed. "Do you want to go with Mercer? He can put you on a plane and take you out of the city. You'll be safe while the EOD hunts the people who took you."

She frowned at him. "Where's the choice?" Her voice was a bit stronger. *Good.*

"You can go where he sends you...or you can come with me. *I* can take you out of the city. I can keep you safe with me."

"Both options have me leaving," Cassidy whispered.

Yes, they did.

But who she left with—

"Going with Cale would be a mistake. He didn't keep you safe before," Mercer's growling voice cut through the room as he stormed inside. He glared at Cale. "She was taken, stabbed, on your watch."

Cassidy sucked in a sharp breath. Cale knew, understood with every fiber of his being, that if Mercer took Cassidy away from him right then, he would never see her again. Mercer would make her vanish.

I can't let that happen.

Cassidy's gaze slid over Cale. To Mercer. "Did you find Genevieve?"

Cale saw Mercer shake his head. Then he glanced at an avid Tina. "Wait outside, Doctor."

Tina hurried to obey. She was probably already afraid that she'd crossed a line with Mercer.

Folks needed to stop jumping when the big, bad wolf growled.

Cale wasn't in the mood to jump.

Mercer waited for the door to shut behind Tina. Then he said, "We found the man you shot."

Cassidy sat up a bit straighter. When she winced, Cale's fingers caressed her arm. He hated for her to hurt.

"H-he can tell you where Genevieve's…body—" she stumbled over that part "—is. You can make him—"

Mercer shook his head. "Doubtful. Dead men don't tell a whole lot."

Cale swore.

"I killed him?"

"Only if you shot him twice, once in the stomach and once in the heart."

Cassidy tried to stand. Cale made sure he gave her the support she needed.

"No. I just shot him once."

"Then it looks like his partner wanted to make sure that he didn't talk. He was left, dead, in the van. Techs are dusting for prints, checking for any evidence that was left behind."

Her breath heaved out. "He knows I'm your daughter. That was why they took me. It had nothing to do with the Executioner, and everything to do with *you*."

Mercer actually backed up a step at the heat in her words. "Cassidy, you need to calm—"

"Calm down? Really? You think that's what I need to

do?" She shook her head. Finally, *finally,* more color came into her face, even if it was in an angry burst across her high cheekbones. "I didn't ask for this life. You're the one who sought it out, not me. I'm just the one who had to pick up the pieces after you."

Silence.

Mercer inhaled slowly. "I have a plane waiting—"

"You always do. Like sweeping me away is going to fix things. This guy *knows* who I am. He knows the secret that we've both tried so hard to cover. If we don't find him, how do we know that others won't discover who I am, too? I've tried your way, Mercer. I've tried it for years." She sounded weary. "I don't want to disappear for you anymore."

Mercer's hard stare cut toward Cale. "And you think you can just walk away with him? That he'll be able to protect you?"

Cassidy's brows rose. "Only recently, *you* thought he could keep me safe. Isn't that the reason you sent him to Rio?"

Mercer's lips thinned. "That was before!"

"Before what?" Cassidy demanded. She still weaved, just a bit, but her voice was much stronger.

"Before I knew he was sleeping with you!"

Cale had been quiet up until that point, but Mercer had just crossed the line. He positioned his body right next to Cassidy's as he faced off against Mercer. "Father or not, you don't use that tone with her—you don't *ever,* understand?"

Mercer stared back at him. Was that shock in his eyes? *Get ready for more.*

"I'm done," Cale said bluntly. He hadn't anticipated saying those words, but he had no choice.

"Done?" Mercer parroted.

"I'm out of the EOD. Consider our test run over."

Definitely more shock now. "You're just going to walk out on Cassidy when she needs—"

"I'm taking her with me. Provided that she wants to come." Cale threaded his fingers through Cassidy's.

Cassidy's lips parted in surprise.

"I told you," he said, focusing just on her. "You have a choice. You can go with Mercer, you can get on his plane, or you can come with me."

"You don't have any place to take her," Mercer snarled. "You don't—"

"Whiskey Ridge isn't more than a spot on the map, but you won't feel hunted there, Cass. My sister and brother-in-law have a ranch. There's plenty of room for us. We can stay there until it's safe for you." *Or for as long as you want. If you like Whiskey Ridge, then I'll buy land for you. For us.*

But he didn't tell her those plans. Not yet. It was too soon. She had enough to deal with at the moment.

"I don't want to put your family in danger," she whispered.

"My brother-in-law was EOD, too. Trust me, he's used to danger." And his brother-in-law, Jasper, knew how to protect what he valued most.

Hope flickered in Cassidy's eyes. "I don't want to be sent away again. I don't want to become someone new."

"You stay yourself, and you come with me."

Now Mercer was the one who wasn't speaking.

"Trust me, Cassidy." Wasn't that what it came down to for them? Her trusting him? Her believing that he was more than just another agent following Mercer's orders?

"I—I do."

Those were the sweetest words he'd ever heard.

"I'll come with you, Cale." She gave him a small smile,

one that made his heart race even faster. He couldn't wait to get her back home.

"You're not making the right choice, Cassidy." Mercer's angry voice.

Only when Cale looked at the EOD director, Mercer's eyes didn't match his voice. No, the expression in his eyes actually looked…pleased.

Like he just played us?

"But if that's your decision, so be it." Mercer hesitated. "I just want you safe."

And he'd been willing to do anything to get her out of D.C. Even use a bit of manipulation?

Would Tina really have gone against him? Or would she have followed his orders—and helped manipulate me, too?

Mercer…always the puppet master.

"Keep her safe, Agent Lane," Mercer ordered.

"I told you, I'm done with the EOD."

"We'll deal with what you are and what you aren't later." Mercer turned for the door. But he didn't open it. His shoulders were ramrod straight, his spine tall. But his voice was a rasp as he said, "I don't want you to wind up like Marguerite."

Cassidy's fingers tightened around Cale's.

"I loved her more than life. I should have made different choices. Maybe it's always about our choices." He glanced back. "I won't make the same mistake."

Then he was gone.

And Cale realized that he had just been well and truly played.

By a master. And a quiet, nervous doctor.

THEY'D GONE BACK to the safe house on Donaghey. Back for a few precious hours before their plane left for Texas.

Cale was inside the place with her, just down the hallway, but Cassidy wanted him closer.

She stared at her image in the bathroom mirror. She looked like hell. Not exactly femme fatale material, but there wasn't much to be done for that then.

Her fingers curled around the doorknob, and a few moments later, the heavy carpet was swallowing her footsteps as she slipped down the hall.

She needed Cale. They were alone, no other guards inside that safe house, and she wanted to be with him.

"Cassidy. Stop."

Cale's voice came from the darkness of the den. How had he even heard her? She'd tried to be so quiet.

"You're hurt." His words were gruff. "Go back to bed. Just rest."

"I don't want to rest." She'd done plenty of that in the hospital, thanks to those ridiculous sedatives. Resting was the last thing on her mind. Cale was what she wanted.

"Cassidy…" Her name was a rough sigh. In that sigh, she could hear need and longing, the same emotions that were rushing through her.

When she was alone, Cassidy thought of all that she'd lost—her mother, Helen, Genevieve. She didn't want to keep thinking of death and fear.

She wanted to think of Cale.

Of pleasure.

She wanted to be reminded that life waited for her. Not just the grim promise of death.

There could be more for her, more for them. Cale wanted her to return home with him. That meant something, didn't it? She was more than a mission to him.

He'd offered to give up the EOD.

That meant—it had to mean—that he felt the way she did.

She took a few more steps toward him.

"I can smell you."

She froze.

"You should smell like the hospital. Antiseptic. Sanitizer…something different…but you're still just like roses. You smell so good. Too good." The lamp flickered on beside him, but instead of illuminating Cale, it just sent dark shadows chasing across the room. His body was a hard outline against the chair. Powerful. She had the fleeting impression of a predator just waiting for his prey to foolishly walk by.

And here I am.

Only she didn't feel like prey.

Cassidy took another step toward him.

She saw his muscles tighten. Saw his hands clench around the arms of the chair.

"*Cassidy.* Where are your clothes?"

Ah, yes, ahem. "I left them in the bathroom." Because not having on clothes would help with the whole seduction routine that she was trying to have going on at that moment.

He lunged from the chair and stood right in front of her in an instant. Stood right there, but he didn't touch her. She needed him to touch her. With the chaos of her life, she *needed him.*

"You're hurt."

The man was sounding like a broken record. "So? We can be careful." Thanks to her dive into the pavement, she'd lost skin on her palms and knees. Her palms had been bandaged, but the tips of her fingers were unharmed. She let her fingertips skim over the powerful muscles of his chest. "I know you can be careful."

His eyes burned down at her.

She rose onto her toes and pressed her lips to his. Her confidence was a brittle thing right then, and when a naked woman offered herself to her lover, well, she expected him to take her up on that offer.

Not stand there, still as stone.

He wants me, doesn't he?

Her tongue slid lightly over his lower lip. Her hips pushed closer against his. Oh, yes, she could feel his arousal. But he wasn't touching her, wasn't kissing her back.

"Cale?" She pulled back just a few inches in order to stare up at him.

"I'm trying to do the right thing," he said, voice gravel-rough in the dark.

Her hero. She smiled. "Can't we forget about right, just for a little while? I want to forget everything—right and wrong—and just be with you." Cassidy kissed him again. His lips had parted, and she dipped her tongue inside that sexy crease.

He growled. The sound rough with desire.

She liked that.

"Don't you want to be with me?" Cassidy asked softly.

Then the room was spinning. No, Cale had just lifted her up, and he was carrying her—holding her so gently— back to the bedroom. He moved quickly, and her heart raced even faster.

He put her on the bed. The mattress dipped beneath their weight. She immediately tried to reach for him.

"No."

The harsh command stopped her. She glared at him in the darkness. Touching him was one of the things she liked the best.

"Sweetheart, if you touch me, I'll go wild."

She was okay with wild. More than okay.

"I have to stay in control. I *can't* hurt you."

Still playing hero. But she thought that was sexy, too.

He spread her arms out on the covers. "Don't move them. Not so much as an inch."

She wasn't about to make a promise that she couldn't keep. Her fingers were already itching to caress him.

But he was caressing her. He'd bent his head, and his mouth—warm, wet—opened over her breast. He licked her. Sucked the flesh, and Cassidy almost came up off the bed.

His hand was on her stomach, sliding lower and lower until he found the heat between her thighs.

He kept licking and kissing her breast even as his fingers stroked the center of her need.

Cassidy tried not to move—she truly did, at first—but her fingers slid away from the covers. She reached for him.

"Remember the rules, Cassidy." His head had lifted. His fingers pressed her wrists back against the covers. "You don't get to move."

"You were hurt, too." She'd seen the bruises on him. The cuts.

"And you're the one that matters more."

Wait, what? That didn't even make any—

His mouth was on her other breast. When he licked her nipple, she could feel the rush of sensual fire go straight to her core. Her hips jerked from the bed, pushing against his. He still had on his jeans, and the rough friction of that fabric was driving her wild.

The man always kept his clothes on too long. Those clothes needed to be on the floor. Cassidy wanted to feel all of him, flesh to flesh.

He was giving her so much pleasure, stroking her with those maddening touches. Using his mouth, those slightly rough fingertips in caresses that were so gentle. Too light.

She didn't need gentle. She just needed him.

"Cale!" The whip of demand had entered her voice.

He eased away from her, ditched his clothes. When he came back to her, the heat from his flesh seemed to scorch her, and it was exactly what she wanted.

Craved.

Their mouths met. She kissed with the frantic need that had built inside her. Let him taste her hunger and desire.

His mouth was harder. More demanding on hers, even as his hands carefully pushed her thighs apart.

So much care…

Then he was between her legs. The heavy ridge of his arousal pressed against her.

She arched toward him.

He thrust into her.

Her nails dug into the covers. Pleasure hit her, cresting over her almost instantly as he withdrew and thrust deeper. Again and again, and she was lost. She gasped out his name and let the release sweep over her.

The thunder of her heartbeat filled her ears, wild and drumming. And Cale was there surrounding her, holding her. Kissing and stroking and making the desire build again. Always, again.

The second time the release hit her, he roared his pleasure, too. Cale stiffened over her, then drove inside her, even deeper than before.

This time, the pleasure wasn't sharp. It was long and consuming. Ripping away the brittle facade that had surrounded her and leaving her feeling exposed, empty—

And very, very much…*his*.

"IT'S TIME TO go, Cassidy."

She smiled at his voice, loving that deep rumble of sound, but Cassidy didn't open her eyes.

She was in the middle of a really good dream. She and

Cale were in a meadow. The sun was shining down on them. They were walking. He had her hand cradled in his.

There was no fear.

No danger.

Just life.

"Sweetheart, we have to go. The car's waiting for us."

His voice was louder now, breaking through the dream. The peace she'd known an instant before began to slip away.

Her eyes opened. Cale stood beside the bed, fully dressed. His expression was carefully guarded, almost blank.

Where was the heat that had blazed before in his eyes? So much passion. A desperate need.

That sensual pleasure hadn't been a dream.

Sweet reality.

"I should have woken you sooner." Now his voice seemed almost hesitant. "But you just looked so…peaceful."

She hadn't exactly enjoyed a lot of peace in her life.

"But we have to hurry. The car's outside."

Right. They were leaving. He was taking her home.

I want to have a home. A real one.

Could Cale give that to her? Did he even know what she wanted from him? Why?

Swallowing, Cassidy turned away from him. Five minutes later, with her hair combed, her teeth brushed and clad in the clothes he'd prepared for her, she was ready to go.

He stayed close while they hurried from the building. Dawn had just come, and streaks of sunlight slid across the D.C. skyline. Gunner was by the vehicle. So was Logan. She glanced to the left and caught sight of—

A flash of red hair.

Cassidy froze.

"Cassidy? What is it?" Cale's hold tightened on her.

Cassidy glanced back at the alley. "Genevieve."

A frown pulled his brows low. "The agents are still searching for her. They'll find—"

"I just saw her." The words were pulled from a throat that suddenly seemed dry. What was happening to her? Was she seeing ghosts? *Seeing what I want to see?*

"Where?" Cale demanded.

She pointed to the alley.

Cale didn't head toward the alley. Instead he guided her to the vehicle. "Make sure she stays inside," he told Gunner.

"What's happening?" Gunner demanded.

"I—I saw…" Wait, *had* she seen her? Cassidy wasn't sure, not anymore. She rubbed temples that ached. "I thought that I saw Genevieve in the alley."

Gunner shook his head. "I cleared that alley. No one is there."

He sounded so certain, but she'd been certain a moment ago, too.

"I'll be right back." Cale pulled his weapon and headed into the alley.

Gunner closed the car door, sealing her inside the vehicle.

Cassidy waited, barely breathing, as the seconds slowly ticked past. Then Cale was back, striding toward the car. His face grim.

He climbed into the vehicle. "No one was there."

Maybe…maybe she'd just wanted Genevieve to be there. Wanted so badly that she'd made herself see a ghost?

The car slowly pulled away from the curb. Helpless to stop herself, Cassidy glanced back.

No one was there.

The car slid easily through the empty streets. Cassidy

swallowed, trying to ease the sudden dryness of her throat. "Did you…did anyone find Genevieve's body?" She hated to think of her friend that way. Broken. Lost.

Cale shook his head.

"Maybe he lied to me." Killers lied, right? That was what they did. Lied, killed.

Cale's fingers caressed her arm. "Maybe he did. Agents will keep searching for her. They won't give up."

Maybe they wouldn't, but… "But I'm giving up. If I'm just running away with you, I'm giving up on her." She couldn't do that. It wasn't right.

"No, you're staying alive." His voice had hardened. They were in the back of the vehicle. Gunner and Logan were up front. The other agents would be able to easily hear every word that they said. "That's what you have to do."

"What if she's in this city?"

Cale shook his head. "What are you going to do? Search every street? Every house? Every building?"

If she had to, maybe. "I can't…I can't do it, Cale." She wanted to, so much, but running—*enough.*

"What can't you do?" He'd leaned toward her.

She dropped her voice to a whisper. "I want to go with you. I want to get on that plane and go home with you. I want to pretend that we're starting some kind of life together, far away from Mercer and everyone else." She licked her lips. "But I can't." Then, voice louder, she focused on the men in the front. "Take us to the EOD headquarters."

Logan didn't even slow down. And he didn't turn around.

"Logan." She snapped out his name. "Take us back."

They eased under a row of bright streetlights—still on because the light of the day wasn't heavy or clear yet—

and, in the rearview mirror, she saw Logan's gaze shift toward Cale.

"It's not his choice," Cassidy said, lifting her chin. "It's mine. And I'm not running."

"Are you dying?" Gunner wanted to know as he glanced back at her. "Because that's what almost happened to you."

Yes, she had almost died, and Cale—no, all of those men—had risked their lives for her.

For her secret.

She opened her mouth and said, "I'm Mercer's daughter."

Wait, had she meant to say that?

Yes.

The silence in the car was heavy. She could feel Cale's gaze boring into her.

"Thank you for all that you've done to protect me," she said, her voice sounding too calm even to her own ears. "But the threats to me won't ever end. They can't. And as much as I want to just run away, to be with Cale…" Her chest was aching. "I can't. I can't leave Genevieve." If there was a chance that her friend was alive, then she had to keep searching for her.

And if Genevieve was dead… *I need to find her body. I can't leave her out there, all alone.*

Gunner was still staring at her. "I know who you are."

"Me, too," came from Logan as the car accelerated.

Cassidy blinked. Well. So much for her big reveal.

"Syd can uncover anything with her computers." Gunner shrugged. "She didn't want me walking in blind in that park, so she made sure I knew."

Cassidy had laid out the puzzle pieces for her. *Because I wanted her to tell him.*

"And you told Logan," Cale muttered to Gunner.

A slow nod from the sniper. "We figured you already knew, seeing how…close…you'd gotten with Cassidy here."

She was grateful for the dark because it hid the heat that stained her cheeks. She and Cale had definitely gotten close.

"I don't see how you being Mercer's daughter changes anything. You and Cale have a plane waiting on you."

They weren't listening to her. "Genevieve could be alive."

Cale's hold tightened on her. "You didn't see her in that alley."

"I'm not so sure about that," Logan said contemplatively.

"What?" Cale's head jerked toward him.

"A few minutes after we left the safe house, a car started tailing us. *Someone* was outside of that place, watching us." His fingers drummed lightly on the steering wheel. "They're staying back, keeping their headlights off, but I still made them."

She immediately spun around, but Cassidy couldn't see anyone following. "Are you sure?"

A rough laugh. "Trust me. I know when I'm being followed."

He would.

"And I know when— *Hell!*" Logan slammed on the brakes, but it did no good because another car barreled right toward them. A big dark SUV that slammed straight into their vehicle. They collided with a crush of metal and the sickening crunch of glass. Cassidy didn't even have the breath to scream as she was thrown forward.

Chapter Eleven

The seat belt cut into Cale's shoulder. Swearing, he yanked it away and reached for Cassidy. "Sweetheart?"

She was pulling on her own seat belt—the belt had jerked her back against her seat. "I'm okay."

"Logan? Gunner?" He snapped out their names.

"My legs are pinned," Gunner growled. "And Logan—"

"Has a gun to his head." A cold, deadly voice floated through the car. A man's voice. A voice Cale had never heard before. He pushed forward to see if the man was bluffing. When he moved, he caught sight of a gun pressed right to Logan's temple. The window on Logan's side had shattered during the crash—or else the guy with the gun had shattered it—and now the man had easy access to the interior of the vehicle.

"Unlock the back doors," that cold voice ordered Logan. "Or I'll put a hole in your head right now and unlock them myself."

Cale pulled his own weapon. When those doors were unlocked, he knew exactly what would happen.

He also knew that Logan *wouldn't* unlock them. Logan was the team leader. He would never sacrifice his team. Even if he had to risk his own life in order to protect them.

"Why don't you get the hell away from me?" Logan invited roughly.

Cale dived for Cassidy, covering her with his body because he could already see Logan moving. Logan's hand whipped up, and the crunch of bones—no doubt the gunman's wrist shattering—filled the car even as a bullet erupted from the weapon.

The bullet flew over the driver's seat, narrowly missing Cale.

The sounds of a struggle came from the front of the vehicle. Cale couldn't help from his current position, so he jumped away from Cassidy, heaved open the back door and—

Genevieve was standing before him. Only she wasn't alone. Another gunman. Another weapon. Only this gun was pressed under her chin.

"Come on, hero," the man—his face covered by a ski mask—said. These thugs sure liked their masks. "Take another step, and she's dead."

Cale didn't move. Not yet. But he planned.

Then Cassidy jumped from the car behind him.

"Cassidy!" Genevieve cried frantically. The woman tried to leap toward her, but the masked man tightened his hold, and Genevieve froze.

The thud of flesh hitting flesh echoed behind them, and in the next moment, Logan was rushing to Cale's side. Cale had known the team leader could handle himself in that fight.

My money is always on Logan.

Now they just had to dispatch this bozo.

"I will kill her right now," the man swore. "I will shoot her while you watch!"

"Then what?" Cale demanded. "We kill you? That's your big exit plan? Death?"

But another vehicle was rushing up behind the armed man, and the guy wasn't even looking over his shoulder.

Since he didn't seem surprised or upset by the speeding car's arrival, Cale knew it could only mean one thing…. *His backup.*

"No, I have another exit plan." The faintest of French accents tinged the man's voice.

The Executioner had been French.

So was Genevieve.

Cale lifted his weapon and aimed at the gunman. "You aren't leaving with her."

"A sniper has you in his sights right now, Mr. Lane."

Was he supposed to be impressed because the guy knew his name?

"If you don't lower your weapon, you'll be dead within the next five seconds."

Bull. He knew better than to believe a line like that.

"Surely you do not think you're the only one who has a sniper on his team?" The gunman shook his head. "Tell them, Genevieve."

"I—I…it's true!" Her voice was high and desperate. "They've been watching you, all of you!"

"We picked this spot. We sprang our trap." The gun dug into Genevieve's chin. "Now we want our prize."

Too bad for them. Cale took a step forward. Cassidy was behind him. He was afraid the woman might try to lunge in front of him and save her friend. He couldn't have that. He couldn't risk Cassidy, not when the end was finally in sight.

His gaze slid toward Logan as he tried to get a read on the other agent's thoughts.

A sniper? If there was a sniper out there, then the best spot for him would be the building on the right. A sniper would have a good position up on the third floor.

But the sniper wouldn't be able to take out both him *and* Logan. If the sniper was even real.

I've heard better bluffs before.

Cale straightened his shoulders. "It's okay, Genevieve. You're going to be fine."

The sun was starting to rise higher. He could see the desperate hope so clearly on Genevieve's face. Hope, but no bruises, no other injuries at all from what he could make out.

Just that wild hope.

"You'll drop your gun?" she whispered.

Cassidy had crept closer to Cale.

Trust me.

He sure hoped that she did.

"This is how it works," the gunman shouted. "You send me the pretty blonde. She gets in that car."

The vehicle had screeched to a stop.

Cale shook his head. "That's not happening." He was adamant.

If Cassidy got in that car, she was dead.

Not going to happen.

Cassidy's fingers pressed against Cale's back.

"You don't make the rules!" the man shrieked, his accent becoming more pronounced. "You don't tell me—"

"It's been more than five seconds," Cale snapped, "and your sniper hasn't fired."

He wasn't there. A damn bluff.

Yet even as he said those words, a man was leaping from the front seat of the backup vehicle. He had a gun clutched in his hands.

Logan fired his weapon instantly, and that man crumpled.

The gunman, the one still trying to hold tight to a now frantically squirming Genevieve, lifted his weapon away from her chin.

That was just what Cale had been waiting for. "Drop!" he yelled.

Genevieve fell.

The gunman brought up his weapon. "No, she's the—" Cale fired on him.

The shot ripped into the man's chest. He stumbled back, gasping, then hit the ground.

Genevieve hunched her shoulders, shuddering. But then the injured man reached for her. He was struggling to rise, trying to get her within his grasp once more.

"Shoot him!" Genevieve begged. "Stop him! Help me!"

His hands were around her. Cale ran forward. He kicked the man back. If he could take the man in alive, then they'd find out exactly who was involved in the plot to abduct Cassidy.

"Kill him!" Genevieve cried. "After what he did to me, make him pay!" She tried to lunge for the discarded gun, but Logan was there, stopping her. He pulled her back and held her in his arms as she cried.

"Genevieve?" Cassidy's hesitant voice. "Genevieve, I am so sorry."

Genevieve looked up at her. Tears slid down her face.

Cale pulled out his phone and called for backup even as he kept his gun aimed on the fallen man.

Cassidy hurried toward Genevieve. "I never meant for you to be hurt."

Genevieve stared at her with glistening eyes. Logan's hands slowly fell away from her.

Logan eased back from the women. Cale saw him turn to make sure that the man in the car wasn't a threat.

It was hard for dead men to be threats.

"You didn't mean…" Genevieve's breath shuddered out. "I know what you meant. I *know*." Then she was hugging tightly to Cassidy, and Cassidy—she was looking straight at Cale.

Thank you. Cassidy mouthed the words as she held her friend close.

Cale nodded. He didn't need her thanks. For Cassidy, he'd do anything.

"Don't worry, Gunner," Logan called as he headed for their car and the trapped EOD agent. "We're going to get you cut out of there."

Yes, they would and—

A bullet slammed into Cale's back. He stumbled as white-hot pain erupted near his spine.

Logan swore. "Shooter! Looked like the shot came from the third—"

A bullet blasted toward Logan. He ducked for cover.

Cale's gun slipped from his fingers when he hit the pavement.

"Cale!" Cassidy screamed.

Then she was there, running her hands over him. Only he couldn't feel her touch.

He couldn't feel anything but that white-hot pain.

"Told you..." Genevieve's voice drifted to him. But it wasn't a voice wild with fear or desperation. It was calm. Cold.

Cruel?

"I told him that a sniper was waiting. He just needed the right signal to fire," Genevieve said in that same cold voice. Cale wanted to see Genevieve's face. But he couldn't see anything then. Not even Cassidy. "I gave him the signal," Genevieve finished, "right when I hugged you."

"You," Cassidy breathed, sounding lost.

"You took something from me, Cassidy, someone that I loved. I thought it was only fitting that you watched while I took away the man that you loved."

Cassidy didn't love him.

Did she?

I love her. But he hadn't told her that. He should have told her. Just like he should have told his parents when they'd dropped him off that day.

They'd dropped him off for practice, driven away. He'd figured he'd see them later.

He'd buried them later.

"Cale, it's okay." Cassidy's fingers swept over his cheek. Gunfire rang out again. The sniper? Keeping Logan in check?

He had to help Cassidy. If he didn't—

"Nothing's *okay,*" Genevieve shouted. "It hasn't been *okay* since you took away Ian. You thought you were so damn clever. You should have been the one to suffer that day, not him!"

He should have seen it sooner. Genevieve hadn't been the victim in Rio. She'd been the accomplice—maybe the accomplice in all of the abductions. The inside man—woman—who'd gotten close to the prey.

Who'd learned their weaknesses, their secrets.

Just like she'd learned Cassidy's.

"He's going to bleed out there. He'll be dead before any help can arrive," Genevieve taunted.

"No!" Cassidy yelled. "He's not!"

More gunfire. *Rat-a-tat.* Only it seemed like—how many people were firing? Two? Three? So much gunfire.

"Step away from him, Cassidy! Come with me now, or I'll put a bullet in his head."

The gun that had been tossed aside…*she* must have it.

"I was going to kill you at the EOD. I was so enraged that day, hurting because you took *Ian!*"

Genevieve had been the shooter? Wasn't she just a woman with some deadly talents.

"But then I realized your death would be too easy. You have to hurt, like I hurt…"

Cale realized exactly what punishment Genevieve had in mind for Cassidy. One lover's life for another.

Cassidy's breath heaved out. She must have realized Genevieve's plan, too, because suddenly she pressed her body flush to his. "Don't leave me," Cassidy whispered to Cale. Then she curled her body around his, protected him.

No. The cry was his, but he couldn't speak.

"Get away from him!" Genevieve's voice was higher. Wilder. But she wasn't shooting.

Because she wants Cassidy alive. Genevieve knew that she could use Cassidy to get to Mercer. *She knows all about the EOD. She's been playing us all.*

A deadly game that was coming to an end.

"I won't leave him!" Cassidy was holding him tightly. Trying to put pressure on his wound, trying to shield him.

"I'll shoot through you!" Genevieve's footsteps scuttled toward them.

A dead daughter couldn't be used against Mercer.

But a live hostage could.

His own weapon was just inches away. He tried to move his hand, but every damn part of him hurt now. The pain was consuming him, sweeping over him in an engulfing wave even as darkness flickered around him.

Too much blood loss. An injury too deep.

A groan broke from him.

"Get away from him!" Genevieve was screaming even louder now, her voice almost breaking. "He dies, just like Ian died. He *killed* Ian, so I'll kill him! Death for death! Death for—"

"Shoot me." Cassidy's voice was coldly quiet. The gunfire had stopped. Had Logan and possibly Gunner managed to take out the sniper up on that third floor? "Shoot me," Cassidy said again. "Because that's what you'll have to do. I won't let you hurt him again!"

"You think I won't?" Genevieve didn't even seem to be aware of the cessation in gunfire. She was too focused on Cassidy.

Was that Cassidy's plan? To distract her?

If so... *Keep it going, sweetheart.*

His fingers moved, just a little. He felt the hard edge of his gun.

"We...we were friends," Cassidy said. Her hair brushed over Cale. She was covering him with her whole body, willing to sacrifice herself for him.

He hadn't thought it would be possible to love her more. He'd been wrong.

"We've been friends for a long time, Genevieve. You don't want—"

"We were *never* friends! You lied to me, always lied." Brittle laughter. "Just as I lied to you. Remember your precious Helen? She begged for you at the end."

Cassidy's body trembled against him. He could feel her now, a bittersweet press of her flesh against his.

"She was such easy prey. So trusting and foolish. They were all easy. I got close to them. I was the one to tell Ian when to take them. I was there—*always* me."

"Why?" Cassidy demanded. She wasn't letting him go.

He wouldn't let her die for him.

"Because I had nothing. I left that boarding school because my family had *nothing*. I was in the street. You were at your parties. Dancing. Drinking. I wasn't going to be thrown away! I was going to have everything!"

Even if she'd had to kill in order to get that life?

"Ian... I met him when I was desperate and alone. He changed me. Helped me."

No, he'd used her, used her connections.

"He taught me how to hunt. Introduced me to his men."

The men she'd still been using as her team. A network that was far bigger than they'd realized. They'd thought that most of the Executioner's men had been killed at that raid in Rio.

Wrong.

"Those men are hiding in the buildings near us right now," Genevieve continued. She was almost on them. He could hear the ragged pull of her breath.

His fingers stretched.

"I will kill you both. All it takes is one wave of my hand. *One wave.* And the bullets will come down on you." More laughter, the cold, uncaring laughter that told Cale she'd let bullets rain down on others before and she hadn't cared.

"You thought you'd fooled me, didn't you, Cassidy?" Genevieve asked. "But it was I all along… I was the better actress. I was the one who played *you*."

The silence chilled him. Logan and Gunner would have attacked by now, if they could have.

It was up to him.

Trust me, Cassidy. He'd told her that before. He hoped she remembered now.

"Leave…" Getting that one word out was so hard.

He knew then how serious his injury was. He wouldn't have much time. He had to make sure Cassidy was safe.

"Run…" When he made his move, she had to run to the car. Had to get inside before any of Genevieve's men fired.

"No." Cassidy's voice was as pain-filled as his own. "If I move, she'll kill you."

But Cassidy had to step back if she hoped to keep living.

"Last chance, Cassidy!" Genevieve's voice rang out. "Get away from your lover! Or you die with him!"

Because she wanted her vengeance. He'd killed Ian, now she thought to kill him.

Think again.

"Get…away…" Cale growled.

"Not happening," Cassidy growled right back at him.

I love her.

"You'd be willing to die for him?" Genevieve screeched. "A man you just met days ago? He doesn't even care about you!"

"I care," was Cassidy's soft response.

Then he heard a thud. Fast, brutal.

It was a sound he'd heard before. A sound he'd made before. The butt of a weapon striking someone.

Cassidy grunted, and he felt her body twist as she turned to fight back against Genevieve.

Genevieve wasn't killing her—she couldn't kill the hostage she wanted—but she was trying to knock Cassidy out. If Cassidy wasn't conscious…

Then you can kill me?

He grabbed for his gun and managed to heave his body to the right.

Cassidy swung out, landing a solid blow to Genevieve's jaw. That wonderful left hook of hers. The redhead screamed, and her hand flew up into the air.

All I have to do is wave.

Did she even realize she'd just given that signal?

"Down!" Logan's roar.

A shot rang out. It sank into Cale's side.

He fired his weapon.

Another weapon fired. The shot seemed to echo, and Cale heard a distant cry.

"Cale?" Cassidy was crouched before him, leaning toward him, her beautiful face surrounded by the darkness that was stretching more with every moment that passed.

He tried to smile at her.

Tears slid down her cheeks.

She knew, he realized. Cassidy already knew just how serious his injuries were.

But there was one thing she didn't know.

"I…love you…" He wished his voice didn't sound so broken, and he wished that he'd told her sooner.

The darkness spread more. Cassidy was the last thing that he saw.

The last, perfect thing.

"CALE!"

His eyes had closed. No, no, he could *not* do this to her. "Help me!" Cassidy shouted.

Then Logan was there, rushing forward with his gun drawn. "Keep pressure on him!"

On the wound at his side or that terrible wound in his back?

His blood was on her hands, soaking her fingers, and fear was like bile in her throat.

"Help's on the way," Logan said. He didn't sound afraid. That meant everything was all right, didn't it? She risked a fast glance at him, but then she saw the fear that flashed in his eyes.

Not all right.

"Cale, please stay with me," she begged him.

But Cale didn't respond because he couldn't.

"I have to make sure that Genevieve is—" Logan broke off, but she understood.

Dead.

Cale's bullet had sunk into Genevieve's chest, even as Genevieve had been lifting her own weapon. Only Genevieve hadn't been aiming at Cale in that last instant. Something had seemed to break in her, and she'd been aiming—

At me.

Cale had stopped her. He'd saved Cassidy. Now he was dying in front of her.

She knew the sniper could fire on them again. She tried to drag Cale's body a few precious inches toward cover.

"It's okay." Logan was back, putting his hands on top of hers. "While hell was breaking loose, Gunner managed to get out of the car. He took out the sniper."

That final shot—it had been Gunner?

"He's checked the area," Logan said. "We're clear."

"Please, don't let him die," Cassidy whispered.

"He won't." Again, his voice was so certain, but she was afraid to look into his eyes.

Cale's eyes were closed. They'd been open and on hers—burning with so much pain—when he'd told her that he loved her.

Then his eyes had closed. Her heart had stopped.

Footsteps thudded toward them. A few moments later, Gunner crouched beside them.

"Did the bullets go through him?" Gunner asked.

Cassidy shivered. "The one at his side…it did. But his back…"

The bullet was lodged in him. She'd seen no sign of an exit wound.

They all stayed crouched over Cale, applying pressure, doing everything they could to save him until an ambulance rushed toward them, lights flashing, siren shrieking.

She'd been taken away in an ambulance before. Cale had stayed with her, every moment.

I love you.

It hadn't been about duty for him. Not about a mission. It had been more. She'd been more to him.

Did he realize that he was everything to her?

"Cassidy!"

That was Mercer's voice, calling out to her. There was emotion, fear, in the cry of her name.

She didn't look toward him. She couldn't look away from Cale.

When he was loaded into the ambulance, she was right there. From now on, wherever Cale was headed, she planned to be *right there* with him.

She didn't even look at her father. She couldn't—her gaze was on the man that she loved.

Mercer was still calling her name when the ambulance sped away.

MERCER WATCHED THE ambulance vanish. Another ambulance. More blood. More death.

Always more.

Cassidy had been crying. Her clothes, her hands, had been stained with blood, and tears had poured silently down her cheeks.

The EMTs were crouched around Genevieve Chevalier's figure now, but there wasn't anything that could be done to save her.

"She's the one," Logan Quinn told him as the agent approached. Other EOD personnel were fanning out, searching the scene. Logan had been clear about where their enemies had been hiding.

Mercer gazed down at Genevieve's form. In all of his years as an agent, he'd learned that evil could hide beneath the most deceptive of surfaces.

It was a lesson his daughter had now learned, too.

"She was going to shoot Cassidy. At the end, she was pointing her weapon at your *asset*." Logan's voice hardened as he delivered that barb.

He knows. Mercer glanced up. Saw that Gunner stood just behind Logan. Gunner was bleeding from about a dozen cuts, but he acted as if he wasn't even aware of the injuries.

"You took her out?" Mercer asked as his gaze stayed on Gunner. Gunner was one of the deadliest snipers that he'd—

"Cale did it." From Logan. Hard. Cold. "Even with a bullet in his back and another bullet driving through his side, he protected Cassidy. *He* saved her."

And Cassidy had been desperate for him. Those tears... Mercer swallowed.

"You didn't count on it, did you?" Logan pressed.

Mercer's breath eased slowly past his lips. "I knew Cale was a good agent. The minute I assigned him to Cassidy's detail, I realized he'd put his life on the line for her."

Logan shook his head. "No, that's not what I meant." A pause. "You didn't realize that they'd fall for each other, did you?"

No.

But they had because on Cassidy's face...there had been grief. Fear. Love.

"What happens now?" Logan wanted to know. "Are you going to try to force her onto another plane? Because, let me tell you, I sure as hell don't think that will happen. She won't leave him. Not unless—" Logan broke off.

But Mercer knew what he'd been about to say. *Not unless Cale dies.*

"Secure the scene," Mercer told him, turning away. He needed to get to that hospital. He needed to get to Cassidy's side. He'd seen Cale's injuries. He knew just how bad they were. If the agent died, then Cassidy would shatter. Mercer knew it because...he'd shattered when Marguerite had died. Shattered and never been able to piece himself back together again.

He couldn't let the same fate fall on Cassidy. She deserved better.

She deserved love. Life.

And he'd give it to her.

He took two steps. Paused. Glanced over his shoulder and made sure that he projected his intent at the two agents. "Whatever you *think* you know about Cassidy Sherridan, you forget it. Got me? After today, you forget everything about her."

With narrowed eyes, Logan glared back at him. "Is that what you do when she's not around? Forget?"

Never.

"Maybe one day you'll understand," Mercer murmured. But, no, he didn't want Logan to understand. Logan had the woman he loved. So did Gunner. He didn't want either man to ever know the pain he felt.

The pain that his daughter was feeling right then.

Because when you lost the other half of yourself, living was near impossible.

"Maybe one day," Mercer repeated. "But pray you don't. Just follow my orders, Agent. Follow them."

And he rushed away, determined to finally be there for his daughter when she needed him.

If Cale dies...

He would make sure that he was there to piece Cassidy's life back together. Somehow.

Chapter Twelve

The operating room doors swung closed, the faint whoosh of sound seeming far too loud for Cassidy's ears.

She stared at those doors, lost. Cale hadn't opened his eyes. Not once during the ambulance ride. He hadn't talked to her again, hadn't squeezed her fingers. He hadn't done anything.

Her hands lifted. His blood had dried on her. She should go wash it off. Her fingers started to shake.

"Cassidy."

She jumped at Mercer's voice, but she didn't turn to face him. "They...they wouldn't let me go back."

Of course not. She knew she couldn't go in surgery. Not with a wound as severe as his. Logically, she understood that, but logic wasn't exactly her strong suit then.

A tear leaked down her cheek. They just wouldn't stop. She swiped her bloody hands over her face. "The doctor said he'd go to ICU after—after he comes out." Because Cale would come out. He'd pull through the surgery just fine. Cale could survive anything. "But only family can see him then."

She wasn't family.

To the doctor, she was no one.

Mercer's fingers closed around her shoulder. Cassidy trembled. She hated for him to see her weak like this. She always tried to put on her strong face when Mercer was around. When your father was a supersoldier, there wasn't supposed to be room for weakness in his daughter.

"I'll get you in that damn ICU room."

Her eyes widened. Mercer's cheeks were flushed, and his eyes were bright with emotion.

"I could get you in that operating room, too, but Cassidy, you don't want to see that. You don't want to see them cutting into Cale."

A scream was breaking inside her, but she clamped her lips together and held it back. When she was sure it wouldn't burst free, Cassidy whispered, "The doctor said… he wanted me to call in Cale's sister because…" It hurt to say it. "Cale might not wake up. His injuries are so bad." Her eyes squeezed shut. "I could see him dying, right in front of me. I couldn't stop it. I couldn't do anything."

Mercer's arms wrapped around her, and he pulled her against his chest. He…hugged her?

She pressed her face against his shoulder. He'd hugged her at her mother's funeral, hugged her just like this. So tightly. As if he never wanted to let her go.

Only he'd pushed her away after that day, pushed her away for so long.

"Your ranger's going to be fine," he promised, his voice gruff. "That man isn't about to give up without a fight. EOD agents are tougher than anyone else out there. He'll pull through."

I…love you.

"He doesn't know," Cassidy told him, her voice a mere breath of sound.

Mercer eased back—just a little—to stare down at her. "Know what?"

"That I love him." It hurt. He'd told her, he'd made sure

that she knew, but she hadn't been able to say those three words to him.

"You'll tell him." Mercer gave a firm nod. "When he comes out of surgery, when he opens his eyes and calls for you, you'll tell him then."

She wanted to believe him. Once, she would have believed anything that Mercer said.

But she wasn't a child anymore. And Mercer's word wasn't law, even if he wanted it to be. "Genevieve planned it all. I thought…I thought I could help her. That she needed me."

"But she was just trying to use you in order to get to me." A muscle flexed along his jaw. "It had to be the agents I sent to guard you. She figured out what—who—you were because of them. She traced them back to me. I put you at risk, the same way I always have. First Marguerite, then you." His hands tightened on her. "I never wanted to hurt either of you."

His voice had broken at the end.

She'd never seen him broken.

"After your mother was killed, I tried so hard, I swear I did. I tried so hard to protect you. But I just made a prison for you—one that you couldn't escape."

Because guards had always been there.

Men and women who'd jumped at Mercer's command. Until Cale.

"I don't know how to open the prison. I don't know what to do."

Mercer didn't know?

"I do." She straightened her shoulders. "You just let me go."

His head bowed. "I want you to be safe." A ragged breath escaped him. "And I want you happy."

She was as far from happy as she could possibly get.

Grief was a knife in her gut, twisting and cutting away at her. The waiting room was empty—just her and Mercer. She had no idea how he'd arranged that. Mercer and his strings.

They sat together. The silence was thick and hard.

She couldn't keep her eyes off those operating room doors. "Tell me again that he'll be okay."

"He will be."

She wanted to believe him. Mercer could move mountains. Once she'd thought her father could make anything happen.

But he hadn't been able to keep her mother alive.

.Cassidy licked her dry lips. "I didn't mean to love him."

"I know." His shoulder brushed hers. "We can't control who we love. You will be able to tell him…soon."

Cassidy nodded, and she prayed that he was right.

CALE HURT. The pain pulsed through him in waves that wouldn't end.

"He's coming around, Doctor. Should we—"

Cale's hand flew out. He grabbed hold of the person talking, and the man's voice broke off.

His throat burned as Cale rasped, "Cass…"

"Sir, we just removed the tube from your throat. You need to calm down."

Forget calm. His hold tightened. His eyelids were heavy, and he struggled to lift them. Had the jerks taped them down? "Cass…"

"Sir, just calm—"

No tape. He finally managed to crack open his eyes. "Want…Cas…sidy…" His voice was stronger, more a snarl than anything else.

The guy he was holding tried to pull free.

"Get…her…"

"Mr. Lane!" Another voice. Snapping.

Was he supposed to be impressed by some doctor's snap?

Need Cassidy. Was she all right? The last thing he remembered was the gunfire.

He'd tried to stop Genevieve before she could hurt Cassidy.

"We just spent hours stitching you back up. You're damn lucky your spine wasn't damaged. Now stop struggling before you undo all my work!"

If they'd get Cassidy, he'd stop. "Cass…"

"Yes, yes, I get it. You need Ms. Sherridan. We'll get her, okay? But first, *calm down* or we'll strap you down."

They'd better not.

He eased his hold on the man. Footsteps raced away.

The doctor's face came into focus as he leaned over Cale. "Mercer told me you'd be like this."

Cale couldn't do more than bare his teeth in a grimace.

"He also told me that you'd pull through, no matter what."

Sinking into that black oblivion of darkness hadn't been an option. Not when he had Cassidy waiting for him in the light.

If she was waiting.

"Don't worry," the doctor told him. "Your Cassidy is fine."

Then the doors flew open and banged against the wall. "Cale!"

No voice had ever been sweeter, even if it was clogged with tears. He turned his head. Saw Cassidy standing in that doorway, with Mercer just a few feet behind her.

Cassidy rushed toward him. Her face was too pale, her eyes too wide. He hated for her to be afraid.

Especially when that fear was for him.

"I'm…okay…"

"He's lucky to be okay," the doctor muttered, plenty loud enough for him to overhear. "If that bullet had been another inch over, he would have—"

Cassidy's lips shook.

"Out!" Mercer's order. "You can tell me outside, Dr. Longtree."

Then Mercer dragged the guy away, barking an order for the male nurse to stay in the room and keep an eye on Cale.

Cale stared up at Cassidy. She was inches away but not touching him. That wasn't good enough. "Closer."

She shook her head. "I don't want to hurt you." But then she crept a little bit closer, as if she couldn't help herself. Her fingers, soft and light, feathered over his arm.

His heartbeat started to calm down. Cassidy soothed him. Cassidy made him feel at peace.

He studied her a moment. Machines were beeping around him, the nurse was trying to blend in with the wall and Cassidy had dried tear tracks on her cheeks. "Is Genevieve…dead?" A blunt question, but one that had to be asked.

"Yes." Cassidy licked her lips. "She's gone."

And he'd been the one to kill her. "She was going to… shoot you. I remember that…. I had to take the shot…."

"What else do you remember?" Her fingers had stilled over his arm.

"The sound of gunshots. A scream." *Cassidy's?*

"Nothing else?"

Was there something? The hesitation in her voice told him that there was.

Her lashes lowered, then lifted so that her gaze could hold his. He loved her eyes—so deep and green and shining with emotion. So—

"You told me that you loved me."

The machines beeped a little louder.

"Cassidy, I—"

"Don't tell me it was the blood loss or delirium or anything like that." Her voice had sharpened. Her eyes narrowed. "Because I'll know that you're lying to me."

He didn't want to lie to her.

Cassidy's shoulders straightened. "You said you loved me because you thought you were going to die, and you didn't want to pass without telling me."

He stayed silent.

She glared. "Next time, don't wait for death, okay? Just *tell me.*"

Uh, okay.

"Because I love you, too, Cale. I love you so much. And when you were bleeding out on that ground, I felt like my world was ending."

He ignored the pain and reached for her, pulled her against him as best he could and kissed her.

Her lips parted for him. Her fingers pressed to his cheek. He could taste the salt of her tears.

And the sweet promise of their future.

"I don't want my world to end," Cassidy whispered. She pulled back a bit to meet his stare. "Cale, I want my life to start again, with you."

He couldn't imagine a life without her. Things between them had developed so quickly—maybe too quickly, but he didn't care. He knew what love was because he'd lived too long without it.

"Whatever we have to do, I'll do it," she promised. "I want to be with you."

He kissed her again. The nurse cleared his throat. "You seem…uh…pretty okay in here. I'll just…step outside a bit."

Cale held tight to Cassidy. Plans, ideas, were racing through his head. Cassidy needed a home base, a place where she could feel safe.

He wanted to give her that—wanted to give her the world.

He would. He'd give her everything. "There's this little town," he whispered. "I mentioned it before, in Texas..."

"Your home."

It hadn't felt like home to him for years, but now, when he thought of her... "Let's take a visit there." See what happened. How she liked it. What she liked.

Because he'd go any place with her—London, Rio, even Whiskey Ridge, Texas.

Wherever Cassidy was happy, that was where he wanted to be.

But Cassidy laughed, a light, husky sound that skipped right through him. He loved it when she laughed. He'd make sure she had plenty of reason to laugh and smile in the years to come.

She was smiling then, flashing the little dimple that he just had to stroke.

"Oh, Cale." Her hand lifted and brushed back his hair. "Don't you understand? Home for me—it's going to be wherever you are. As long as we're together..."

They would be. Together for the rest of their lives.

"Then I'm happy," she finished.

He gazed at her, completely lost for a moment. His society girl, his fierce fighter.

His.

The woman he'd cherish for the rest of his days.

"I love you, Cassidy Sherridan."

Her smile widened.

Protecting her had been the best assignment of his life.

He'd owe Mercer for that, for connecting him with the woman of his dreams.

Cale was sure Mercer would come collect on that debt. The guy always did.

But that didn't matter. The only thing that mattered—she was in his arms.

The place where he always wanted her to be.

Cale kissed her again.

They were both home.

MERCER TURNED AWAY from the hospital door, but Cassidy's quiet words still rang in his ears. *When you were bleeding out on the ground, I felt like my world was ending.*

He knew exactly how his daughter felt.

But Cassidy's world wouldn't end. She'd have her man, and they'd be together. Cale was a fighter, a protector—that was why Mercer had recruited him for the EOD. And it was also why he'd sent Cale down to guard Cassidy.

I'd thought, hoped...

And his plan had worked. Cassidy would now have a warrior by her side, day in and day out. A man willing to put his life on the line for her.

More plans would have to be made. Cassidy wanted out of her prison. He had to find a way to make that happen. He'd have to figure out a way to clear her so that his enemies wouldn't hunt for her any longer.

Had Genevieve leaked the information that she'd had? Sold it to any of her and Ian's connections? He'd find out, and he'd eliminate any threats to his daughter.

He might have to use some bait, might have to call in some old favors, but he *would* give Cassidy her freedom.

Mercer had lost his chance at love, but he'd make sure that his daughter had her happiness.

She deserved it.

He began to whistle as he walked down the hallway, plans and schemes running through his mind.

Cassidy was going to be free.

And she'd have the life that she'd always wanted.

No matter what, he'd make the dream happen for her, even if it meant he had to get his hands a little bit bloody.

After all, the EOD was used to blood and death.

He *was* the EOD. He had this.

Epilogue

She wasn't in a ballroom anymore. She wasn't wearing a glimmering green gown that matched her eyes.

She wore jeans, a faded T-shirt.

She was standing in a meadow, laughing.

Cale's arms were crossed over his chest as he stared at Cassidy. They'd been in Whiskey Ridge for two weeks—just two short weeks—and Cassidy seemed to glow with happiness.

She didn't wake up afraid that one of her father's enemies would find her. She slept through the nights, held carefully in his arms.

They watched sunsets together. Rose at dawn to see that same sun rise.

They made love.

They talked about the future.

And he dreamed of everything that he wanted to give her.

Because that was what she'd already given to him.

She's every damn dream I ever had.

Cassidy glanced over at him, and she smiled. Her dimple flashed. His heartbeat kicked up.

Slowly, she strode toward him. "Hi, there, cowboy."

The title had been mocking once—still was their own

joke. The cowboy and the princess. That was how he thought of them.

Two different worlds. They probably should have never been together.

But they were.

When he'd finally been released from the hospital, Cale hadn't been able to get her home soon enough.

And this place…with her there, it truly felt like home.

"I'm happy here," Cassidy said, the words simple. *True.* No telling hitch gave away a lie.

She didn't lie anymore or, at least, not to him. That hitch had sure slipped through when she'd gamely tried his sister's roast beef the day before.

"Could you always be happy here?" he asked her carefully.

Her hands rose. She stroked his face, her fingertips lightly smoothing over the stubble that lined his jaw. "I told you before, I'm going to be happy as long as I'm with you. And I don't care where we are."

As long as they were together.

He held her gaze and slowly dropped to one knee.

"Cale?"

He opened the box in his hand. Before he'd left D.C., he'd picked up one very special item. He opened the box.

A diamond wasn't nestled inside.

An emerald was. One that reminded him perfectly of her eyes.

Those eyes were very wide right then.

"Cassidy Sherridan, will you do me the honor of becoming my wife?"

She just stared at him.

Oh, hell. He should have gone with the diamond. Getting the emerald had been a bad idea. It was just—

She yanked him to his feet. Kissed him hard and deep

and wild. He could taste her love and her passion and all the sweetness that was his Cassidy.

"Yes," she whispered against his lips. "Yes!" That time, she shouted her answer.

And he laughed and held her tighter.

Sometimes, dreams did come true—even the broken dreams of an ex-mercenary.

"Like I was going to let you get away," Cassidy whispered, giving a small shake of her head. "Not happening." Then she sobered as she stared at him. "It's not every day that a man is willing to die for me."

And it wasn't every day that he was given something special to live for—someone special.

His Cassidy.

"I hope the wedding's soon," she told him, and a wicked glint had entered her eyes.

"Sweetheart, it will be as soon as you want."

He was ready for their forever to start—a lifetime of love and happiness. No more fears.

And no more nightmares for Cassidy.

He'd make sure the rest of her days were as good as this one.

He kissed her again and knew that life couldn't get any better.

* * * * *

REQUEST YOUR FREE BOOKS!
2 FREE NOVELS PLUS 2 FREE GIFTS!

◆ HARLEQUIN®

INTRIGUE®

BREATHTAKING ROMANTIC SUSPENSE

YES! Please send me 2 FREE Harlequin Intrigue® novels and my 2 FREE gifts (gifts are worth about $10). After receiving them, if I don't wish to receive any more books, I can return the shipping statement marked "cancel." If I don't cancel, I will receive 6 brand-new novels every month and be billed just $4.74 per book in the U.S. or $5.24 per book in Canada. That's a savings of at least 14% off the cover price! It's quite a bargain! Shipping and handling is just 50¢ per book in the U.S. and 75¢ per book in Canada.* I understand that accepting the 2 free books and gifts places me under no obligation to buy anything. I can always return a shipment and cancel at any time. Even if I never buy another book, the two free books and gifts are mine to keep forever.

182/382 HDN F42N

Name _____ (PLEASE PRINT)

Address _____ Apt. #

City _____ State/Prov. _____ Zip/Postal Code

Signature (if under 18, a parent or guardian must sign)

Mail to the Harlequin® Reader Service:
IN U.S.A.: P.O. Box 1867, Buffalo, NY 14240-1867
IN CANADA: P.O. Box 609, Fort Erie, Ontario L2A 5X3

Are you a subscriber to Harlequin Intrigue books and want to receive the larger-print edition?
Call 1-800-873-8635 or visit www.ReaderService.com.

* Terms and prices subject to change without notice. Prices do not include applicable taxes. Sales tax applicable in N.Y. Canadian residents will be charged applicable taxes. Offer not valid in Quebec. This offer is limited to one order per household. Not valid for current subscribers to Harlequin Intrigue books. All orders subject to credit approval. Credit or debit balances in a customer's account(s) may be offset by any other outstanding balance owed by or to the customer. Please allow 4 to 6 weeks for delivery. Offer available while quantities last.

Your Privacy—The Harlequin® Reader Service is committed to protecting your privacy. Our Privacy Policy is available online at www.ReaderService.com or upon request from the Harlequin Reader Service.

We make a portion of our mailing list available to reputable third parties that offer products we believe may interest you. If you prefer that we not exchange your name with third parties, or if you wish to clarify or modify your communication preferences, please visit us at www.ReaderService.com/consumerschoice or write to us at Harlequin Reader Service Preference Service, P.O. Box 9062, Buffalo, NY 14269. Include your complete name and address.

HI13R

SPECIAL EXCERPT FROM

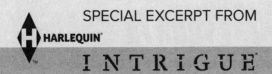
HARLEQUIN®

INTRIGUE®

Read on for a sneak peek of
READY, AIM… I DO!
by USA TODAY *bestselling author*
Debra Webb
Part of the Colby Agency: The Specialist series.

*On secret orders, Colby Agency specialist Jason Grant is
sent to Las Vegas to rescue a spy whose cover has been
compromised. Everything appears to be routine…until
he wakes up married to the gorgeous woman he was
sent to save.*

He reached for the glass of water on the nightstand and
stopped dead. The wide gold band on the ring finger of his
left hand glinted in the sunlight. He rubbed at his eyes, but
it didn't go away. He was married?

His head and stomach protested as he took in the strewn
clothing along with this new information.

No. Impossible. No way he'd forget his own wedding or
the inevitable events leading up to it. No way he'd marry a
stranger—and Ginger Olin, CIA operative, fit that description.
This had to be some ruse she'd invented to preserve her cover.

He couldn't make sense of the vague scenes flitting through
his mind. She owed him some answers. This time when he
pushed to his feet, he kept moving forward despite the sudden
tilt of the room. He was grateful when the wall kept him from
hitting the floor. He pounded a fist on the bathroom door. "Get
out here."

HIEXP1013

She opened the door and a steamy cloud of spicy vanilla scent washed over him.

"Oh, dear," she said with a sly smile as her gaze slid over his body like a touch. One long fingertip trailed across his jaw. "You're looking rough." She opened the door wider. "Come on in. A shower will fix you right up."

Was that a bit of Irish in her voice this morning? If so, was it real? He'd done a little investigating after their last meeting and knew she had a talent for accents.

She tucked herself under his arm, keeping him steady as she walked him past the long vanity. Something about the gesture felt familiar.

"Did you do this last night?"

"We can talk about last night when your head's clear." She eased back but didn't quite let go. "Steady?"

Barely. "Yes."

"Cold or hot?"

"Pardon?"

"The shower," she clarified, her eyes quickly darting down to his groin and back up again.

"Cold."

"All righty."

The secrets are only just starting.
Find out what happens next in
READY, AIM...I DO!
by USA TODAY *bestselling author*
Debra Webb

Available September 17, only from Harlequin® Intrigue®.

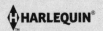

HARLEQUIN®

INTRIGUE®

THE STAKES ARE HIGHER AND THE DANGER IS BIGGER IN

MY SPY
BY DANA MARTON

A mission gone wrong forced injured soldier Jamie Cassidy to start anew…and run right into the path of deputy sheriff Bree Tridle. The sassy, sexy Texan was as determined to uncover a local money-laundering scheme as Jamie was to keep her safe from the stalker hot on her trail. When a deadly attack on Bree's home escalates the danger *and* their attraction, they must face their enemies together to save not only their country, but their one chance at love.

2 NOVELS for the **PRICE** of **1**

LAST SPY STANDING
also included in this book!

*Available September 17, 2013,
only from Harlequin® Intrigue®.*

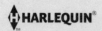

HARLEQUIN®

INTRIGUE®

THE LAST THING MIRANDA LEWIS REMEMBERS IS BEING SHOT....

When a sexy blue-eyed stranger finds her, she has no memory of who she is or what she's doing in the jungles of Colombia.

Gage Booker risked his life in the raid on the compound, only to discover his quarry gone and an injured woman left for dead, a woman the covert operative would be a fool to trust. But her amnesia seems real—and so does the passion exploding between them.

TRAP, SECURE

BY CAROL ERICSON

2 NOVELS for the PRICE of 1

NAVY SEAL SECURITY
also included in this book!

*Available September 17, 2013,
only from Harlequin® Intrigue®.*